AF071220

Forever In Time

Nicky Charles

Ingram Hardcover Revised Edition

Canadian grammar was used in this book, hence you might notice some punctuation and spelling variations.

Edited by Jan Gordon
Line edits by Moody Edits

Cover Design by Nicky Charles
Cover Photos © Thinkstock.ca
Hourglass image used with permission
from Mihaela "Detonatress" Dragusin
Hourglass watermark and logo by Jazer Designs

ISBN: 978-1-989058-11-4

This book is dedicated to

Jan Gordon

It was an idle conversation while reviewing her book, Black Silk, that inspired this story. Without that comment (which she doesn't even recall making, lol) I never would have attempted to write original fiction.

I'd also like to mention Cheryl who allowed me to join 'Wicky' and encouraged me to share my stories, and Ermintrude who first offered to read over my initial rough scribbles of this tale.

Prologue

March 1938, Scotland

Ivan stood as tall and proud as always, despite his seventy-five years. His dark hair, now liberally sprinkled with grey, was highlighted by the faint mist that fell over the cold, windswept cemetery. It was a typical March day. The trees were still bare and the grass was brown. Only the occasional green shoot poked its head up to offer hope of better days to come.

Listening to the drone of the minister's voice, he absentmindedly watched the little white puffs of vapour that appeared with each breath the man took. The minister meant his words to be comforting, offering hope and solace, but in actuality, they just washed over him, bringing no real relief. His heart beat heavily in his chest, his throat was tight from emotions held firmly in check. It was ridiculous to feel this way; he'd known the inevitable would happen, but the knowledge hadn't made reality any easier to bear. She was gone. His beloved wife of fifty-three years was dead.

They'd had a wonderful life together, with four children and twelve grandchildren. When they'd immigrated to Scotland from Russia, it had been hard. Natalia had hated leaving her family behind, but he'd sensed the growing political unrest and knew they needed to find a better place to raise their family. Scotland had been good to them. Their home, while simple, had not lacked for the necessities; love and laughter had filled the rooms. A fire had almost always burned in the hearth, while the kettle simmered on the stove, ready to make a pot of tea for anyone who happened to stop by for a visit.

Of course, the children were grown now with their own families and the house had become much quieter in recent years, but as long as his wife had been by his side, it hadn't mattered. However, now that she was gone, the rooms echoed strangely as he walked through them. It had only been two days since she had died, but already the house seemed less inviting, the smell of her cooking and the scent of the perfume she had so loved, were already fading away. At night his bed was cold and lonely. There was no one holding his hand as he drifted off to sleep, no one kissing him awake in the morning. With a sigh, he realized that was all over. He had no home now; no one to be his other half. No reason to continue with this life.

"Dad? It's time to go." His eldest son, Daniel, touched his shoulder and he started. Looking around, he realized the others had gone. He hadn't even noticed. Glancing down, he wiggled his fingers, discovering that they were warm and slightly damp from having shaken the hands of family and friends. His wife had been liked in the community. Many had stopped to offer their condolences before leaving the cemetery. Had he even responded to their well-meant words? He hoped so. Natalia wouldn't have wanted him to be rude; she'd always been a stickler for manners.

Looking at his son, he met his concerned gaze and gave a brief nod before starting to walk towards the car. His daughter-in-law, Mary, stood beside the vehicle holding the hand of three year old Sarah, the youngest grandchild. The girl looked just like her grandmother, and he felt the faintest of smiles appear on his face at the sight of the toddler bouncing up and down beside her mother.

"You will come back to our house, won't you?" Mary asked.

He hesitated. They were trying to be kind, but in reality all he wanted was some time alone to think about the past and to plan his future. Behind him he heard the dull thud of dirt falling on the wooden casket. A shiver ran through him. His fists clenched and he closed his eyes trying to block out the thought of his lovely wife, now lying stiff and cold in the ground. Maybe today was not the day to be by himself after all. The pain was still too fresh. It wouldn't hurt to let himself be surrounded by the warmth of his family for a little while longer.

"All right, I'll come, but just for a while." His voice sounded gruff, even to his own ears, but Mary just smiled and wrapped her hand around his upper arm. "I'll help you into the car. Do you mind if Sarah sits with you?" Without waiting for his reply, the little girl was placed on his lap. She immediately snuggled her golden head against his chest and grinned up at him, her blue-green eyes sparkling—Natalia's eyes.

~~~

July 2009, USA

Stephanie Fields sat inside the stylish hair salon biting her lip as the hairdresser cooed over her straight strawberry blond hair.

"It's a lovely colour," the woman gushed. "But the length is all wrong. A shorter style will give it more body and," she pulled the long tresses back, "if we shorten it near your face like this, those blue-green eyes of yours will really stand out."

"See?" Paula, her best friend, stood beside her smiling. "Isn't that what I'm always telling you?"

Steph nodded, trying to hide her apprehension as she studied the stylist's image in the mirror. The woman's hair was cropped in a short boy-cut on the right with a longer fringe on the left. The fringe had rainbow coloured highlights.

The cut and style were Paula's birthday present to her. Ever since the trendy new spa had opened across the street from the flower shop Stephanie owned, Paula had been urging her to use the service. While Stephanie appreciated the gesture, she wasn't so sure it was a good idea. Cutting her long hair was a big step and change wasn't something she embraced easily. She liked things to be stable and thought each step through before taking it. Even selecting a new breakfast cereal could leave her standing in the grocery store aisle for ages as she debated the pros and cons of various choices. It drove people crazy, she knew that, but she just wasn't the spontaneous sort. Every action had a consequence, and she had to be sure she could live with the results of her choices.

Paula must have seen the doubt in her eyes and began to encourage her even more.
~~~

"Come on, Stephanie. You've had long, straight hair ever since I've known you. Getting an inch off the ends doesn't qualify as a new style. It's your birthday. Live a little." Paula was a perky, dark haired, ball of energy, the total antithesis of her best friend and boss.

While Paula was short, curvy and outgoing, Stephanie was tall, slim and reserved. Paula embraced life and new experiences, while Stephanie tended to sit on the sidelines observing. People were often surprised to find they were best friends, but they were, each having characteristics that complemented the other. Stephanie reined Paula in from some of her more outlandish schemes, and Paula kept Stephanie from being a complete stick-in-the-mud.

Right now, her friend was urging her to take a walk on the wild side—well, at least what Stephanie considered wild.

Well… I suppose." She began to cave under the urgings. Maybe she should get it cut. It was just hair after all, and perhaps a change would be good. It might even perk up her spirits after the string of bad luck she'd been having lately.

Almost every day for the past two weeks, she'd been plagued by one problem or another. Last Monday she'd had a flat tire and, after getting it repaired, had managed to run over a nail the very next day. On Wednesday, in the middle of making deliveries, she'd run out of gas, even though she was sure she had at least a quarter of a tank. Her dry cleaning had disappeared from her car on Thursday and, over the weekend, a dog had walked all over her newly planted petunias. To top it all off, the air conditioner at her house had died in the middle of the summer heat wave.

Yes, definitely a string of bad luck.

She sneezed and that reminded her of yet another issue. She'd developed an allergy of some sort, and the pills she was taking for the symptoms weren't doing any good. The only effect the medication seemed to be having was to make her brain fuzzy and give her a slight case of paranoia. At times, she was sure there was a voice echoing in her head, and she could swear someone was watching her, which was utterly ridiculous. A person as boringly ordinary as herself would never warrant close observation.

"Come on, Steph. Just say 'yes' to the cut." Paula's voice brought her back to the matter at hand. A new style. Was it time for a change?

She took a deep breath and made her decision. "All right. Cut away. As you said, it will grow back."

Paula literally bounced with pleasure. "Steph, you're going to love this look, I just know it! And who knows, this might be the first step to a whole new life!"

Stephanie smiled wanly at her, clenching her hands beneath the protective cape the stylist had draped over her. At least one of them was happy.

Chapter 1

Jake sat in his car intently watching the building across the street. He drummed his fingers lightly on the steering wheel, keeping time with the music playing softly on the radio. It was an old tune from the 1980's about an obsessive stalker who watched every move made by the target of his affection. He allowed a faint smile to break the impassivity of his face at the irony of the song. Yes, he was watching and not a single move escaped his attentive eyes. Cars occasionally passed by, momentarily obscuring his view, but these minor inconveniences were to be expected; such was the human condition.

A breeze blew in the open window, briefly cooling the interior of the vehicle. It was mid-July and the summer heat was making itself known. The vinyl seats of his non-descript, black car were hot and his shirt stuck to his back, while little rivers of sweat trickled down his neck.

Shifting slightly into a more comfortable position, he never took his eyes off his target. Instead, he reached out for the can of pop in the cup holder to his right, finding it by touch alone. He took a swig of cola, grimacing slightly at the taste. The liquid was warm and flat, doing little to quench his thirst. He could go to the corner store and buy something cold, but then he'd have to abandon his surveillance and that was unacceptable.

While acknowledging the physical effects of the heat on his body, he chose to ignore them. Neither the heat, nor the cold, impinged on him to any great extent. He simply pushed such bothersome details to the side.

Stephanie was in that building. He knew it. He'd followed her that morning as she left her house, keeping a discreet distance, doing nothing that could alert her, or anyone else, of his intentions. After stopping at the drug store, she'd made her way here, to the flower shop. Several times he'd seen her pass by the window as she went about her job, blissfully unaware of his presence outside. The angle of the sun made it difficult to see into the building, but her bright coral top was hard to miss. Intermittent flashes of colour could be seen through the window as she moved about and were sufficient to keep his attention riveted. Eventually she would have to come out.

Time was on his side.

He could wait.

Wait until his target appeared.

In his mind he could see her. Every detail of her body was as familiar to him as his own. She was slightly taller than average, but he knew her head would still tuck under his chin. Her body was slim rather than curvaceous, but nicely rounded where it mattered. A dusting of freckles scattered over her nose, and there was a moon-shaped birthmark on her upper left thigh.

Carefully, he picked up the picture of her from the seat beside him and rested it on the steering wheel. Keeping one eye on the flower shop, he glanced at the photo, tracing his finger over her features. It hadn't been necessary to bring the picture along. He'd never be able to forget what she looked like. However, having it with him made her seem closer as he bided his time, waiting until they would finally be together. It was his favourite photo from his collection.

The picture was candid, taken while she was talking with a customer. Her blue-green eyes were wide, and a polite smile adorned her full lips. He knew just how those lips would feel under his. They'd be soft and yielding, hesitant at first, but then eager once she finally realized their mutual passion. The tip of his tongue slid out, wetting his own lips, anticipating that moment.

Her hair in the picture was long, but just recently she'd had it cut into shoulder-length layers. He admitted that it suited her, but mourned the loss of her long strawberry blond tresses. The longer hair had figured heavily in his fantasies, and he was loath to abandon visions of it trailing over his body or having it wrapped around his wrists while he held her captive to his whim. It was a shame, but he shrugged philosophically. The hair was gone now, but she'd grow it back for him, once she realized his preference.

He wondered what it would be like when she finally said his name. Her voice was slightly husky and sent shivers of excitement through him whenever he heard it. Once he'd called her at home and just listened to the sound of her saying hello over and over, before finally hanging up. He'd only done it that one time, and had immediately regretted his actions. Phone calls with no one on the other end would only make her nervous and wary. He didn't want that.

Instead, when the need to hear her voice became too much to resist, he'd follow her through the mall, listening to her talk to store clerks and fellow shoppers. He was always careful that she never sensed his presence, moving away if he felt she might have noticed him. In restaurants, he'd sit at nearby tables or adjoining booths, never looking her way, just listening to the sound of her laughing with friends. He loved to hear her laugh. Her happiness was all he ever wanted. Soon, she'd realize that.

There was a slight tapping on the roof of the car and he started, turning to stare at a middle-aged woman holding a handful of flyers.

"Excuse me, sir. I'm sorry to bother you..."

"No bother at all, ma'am." He spoke slowly and calmly, trying to give no indication of his inner frustration at having been disturbed. "How can I help you?"

"Well, I'm just distributing these flyers, tucking them under the wipers of all the cars, but since you're in yours, it seems sort of silly to not just hand it to you."

"I totally agree. What's the flyer for?" He gave her a smile and she flushed. Over the years, he'd learned the power his smile had over women and used it unashamedly.

"Our church is holding a spaghetti dinner fundraiser next weekend. We're trying to make enough money to build a new roof."

"Good idea. Here." He reached into his pocket and pulled out his wallet, extracting several bills.

"Oh no, sir! I'm not selling tickets, just telling you about the event." She stammered as he pressed the bills into her hand.

"I may or may not be able to make it to the dinner." He infused his voice with regret. "Please. Take the money as a donation."

"Well, thank you, sir. May God bless your kind soul."

He nodded and smiled at the woman once again, then watched her walk away through his rear-view mirror. 'Bless his soul?' Did he even have a soul? Somehow he doubted it.

His wallet was still in his hand and had fallen open to his driver's licence. He studied it for a moment, refreshing his memory as to the particulars of his 'life'. It proclaimed him to be Jacob St. Clair, thirty years old, six feet two inches in height and weighing one hundred seventy five pounds. The picture was a decent likeness, showing his black hair and blue eyes. Smirking, he recalled how the girl at the desk had fussed over him, eagerly helping him replace his 'ruined' licence. She'd easily bought his story of accidentally washing and ironing his old one...

"I think it's wonderful that a man is domesticated enough to iron."

Knowing that she was throwing out hints, he played along. Leaning on the counter, he gave a negligent shrug. "I live alone. I have to know how to take care of myself."

"Alone?" Her demeanour changed from merely helpful to predatory interest.

"Yes. In fact, I've just recently moved to town." He allowed a smile to curl the corner of his mouth.

"Really? And what brings you to Weston?" She started paying more attention to him than the information she was typing into the computer.

"I'm a financial advisor and I'm planning on setting up a private investment firm. There seems to be a niche for one in this area."

It was, after all, roughly the truth. He had investments; they were just all his own. Long ago, he'd found out that keeping his stories only a few degrees off reality made them more plausible and easier to remember. Even the changes he'd slipped into his licence application had been minor. Unrepentantly, he'd used his wide friendly smile and a generous dose of charm to distract the woman from noticing the alterations. It worked, just as it had every time before. Cynically, he acknowledged that being considered a 'hunk' helped when establishing a new identity.

It was a fine line that he walked, intermixing legal and forged documentation of his life, but it was a formula he'd perfected and used successfully for years. All it really took was one credit card, or a library card, to start the ball rolling. After that, everything else typically fell into place.

He'd rented a pre-furnished apartment, set up a bank account and even had a membership at a local gym. His body was lean and muscular by nature, but it never hurt to be seen walking around with a gym bag. It added to the 'normal' aura he was trying to establish in town. So far it seemed to be working. He flipped the wallet shut and put it away, focusing his attention on the flower shop once again.

A glance at his watch showed that it was almost one-thirty. Stephanie would be leaving soon. He knew her schedule by heart and could predict the pattern of her day. Tuesday was her short shift at work. She'd leave, go to the library, then the grocery store and possibly complete a few other errands before heading home. Once there, she'd feed the cat, change her clothes, make herself a salad for supper and spend the rest of the evening reading and eating chips and dip. Smiling, he recalled a conversation he'd overheard between her and a friend; how she justified the chips and dip by eating just a salad for dinner.

Suddenly, he sat up, all of his senses alert.

Yes, there she was, leaving the store and walking diagonally across the road to the library. He cringed when a car turned the corner and she had to quicken her pace to avoid being hit. Crossing at the light would have to be one of the talks they'd need to have. Reckless behaviour couldn't be tolerated. The thought of her being injured or, worse yet, killed while crossing the street would have had him breaking out into a sweat, if the summer heat hadn't already accomplished the job. He'd waited too long to lose her now.

Soon, she left the library, a stack of books in her arms. He knew they'd be romance novels of various types, some historical, some paranormal, a few that were risqué. When he'd found the smutty ones in her house, he'd been delighted rather than offended. Her interest in sex tantalized him, making him long for her all the more. Even now his body hummed, just thinking of her reading the erotic passages, her heartbeat increasing slightly, her body possibly readying itself for an imaginary lover.

"I could ease that ache for you," he murmured while shifting in his seat.

He watched her get into her car and pull out of the parking lot, heading towards the local grocery store. He followed at a discreet distance, parking two lanes over. Briefly, he debated following her inside; he could watch her bite her lip as she debated the merits of grapes over cantaloupe, but he'd done that last week and she'd almost noticed him staring. Luckily, a mother with two fussing children had come down the aisle and she'd looked away, no doubt forgetting about the dark-haired stranger who had been watching her.

No. He couldn't risk it. The timing had to be just right. Everything had to be perfect. For ages, he'd been planning this, and the cheap thrill of watching her buy groceries wasn't worth it. Instead, he'd bide his time. He'd watch from afar, comforted by the knowledge that soon it would be time for her to meet her fate.

"I'm waiting for you Stephanie," he whispered as she exited the grocery store and put her purchases into her sensible grey car. "I've been waiting a very, very long time."

Chapter 2

"Another hot day."

Stephanie nodded in agreement at the idle comment made by an unknown shopper. Their paths crossed as she exited the store and the man entered.

"Sure is." She adjusted the grocery bags she was carrying and proceeded to make her way to her car.

Waves of heat shimmered above the pavement and the sun glared off the windshields of the parked vehicles. The breeze was hot and did little to provide relief from the scorching temperatures. Stephanie thought longingly of the carton of ice cream she'd bought, imagining how the cold treat would feel as it melted in her mouth and slid down her throat. In the midst of all this heat, it would be like a bit of heaven.

Anticipating eating the ice cream, she quickly finished packing her groceries into her car while throwing out a prayer that it wouldn't melt too much on her way home.

As she shut the trunk and rounded her vehicle to the driver's door, the skin on the back of her neck prickled and a vague sense of unease washed over her, almost as if she were being watched. She paused and surveyed the area, slowly turning in a complete circle.

Rows of cars were on either side of her, their metallic surfaces glinting in the sun light. From what she could see, the vehicles were all empty and the parking lot was devoid of shoppers as well. The road, just yards away, had only light traffic and cars whizzed by, the drivers giving no sign of noticing her presence. She tucked her hair behind her ears and exhaled slowly, trying to get rid of the feeling of paranoia. It was just her imagination combined with the effects of those darned allergy pills making her brain a bit muzzy.

She climbed in behind the wheel and started for home, still trying to justify her feelings. Déjà vu often plagued her, but this sense of being watched was new. No doubt it was her recent run of bad luck playing on her nerves and causing her to start at shadows. She was tense, just waiting for the next irritating occurrence.

Of course, the hot, humid weather wasn't helping either, making sleeping difficult. Strange dreams, filled with voices calling her name, punctuated what little sleep she managed to achieve, leaving her groggy during the day. Surely, she reasoned, that in itself was enough to put one's equilibrium off.

The drive home was thankfully uneventful, and she pulled into the driveway and parked the car. Her home was a small, roman brick building with black shutters and white trim. Several small shrubs decorated the front yard and a pot of geraniums sat on the front step. It was a simple house but it was hers, and she loved it.

Knowing the ice cream was likely melting, she quickly lugged the groceries up to the door and fumbled for her key. Inside, Coco, her cat, was meowing pathetically, sensing her presence and eager for dinner. When the door opened, the feline tried to slip out, but months of experience had Stephanie deftly blocking the cat with her foot and pushing her back inside.

"No you don't. You're an inside cat now, remember?" She spoke sternly to the furry little beast, which she'd rescued several months ago. While Coco was undoubtedly grateful for her steady diet and comfortable home, she still seemed to want to roam freely through the neighbourhood.

Stephanie pushed the door shut with her hip, and put the groceries on the kitchen table. After popping the ice cream in the freezer, she pulled out a can of tuna for the cat. Tuesday was treat night both for her and her pet. Coco jumped onto the counter, whirling and twirling in front of her mistress.

"You're not helping any by doing that," Stephanie laughed as a tail brushed across her face. She gently pushed the cat to the side and talked to the feline while dishing out her food. "See? If I'd let you outside, you'd be missing this wonderful dinner. Instead, you'd be eating scrawny sparrows and garbage from the cans in the alley."

She picked up the tortoiseshell cat and looked her in the eye. "Besides, I took you to the vet. You've had all your shots and you've been spayed. You have absolutely no need to roam about looking for male companionship. All that would happen outside is that you'd probably get in a fight, dig up someone's flowers and terrorize the wildlife."

Coco blinked at her as if to say, 'And what's wrong with that?'

Stephanie laughed at the expression on the animal's face and set it down, placing the dish of food within easy reach.

Leaving the cat to enjoy its meal, she went to change into something more comfortable. A pink tank top and a pair of grey shorts seemed just the thing. The air conditioning was still broken and the house was warm and stuffy. After debating for a moment, she ditched her bra. She was home alone; no one would see her.

Feeling much more comfortable, she headed back to the kitchen.

Having finished the tuna, Coco was now vigorously washing up. The cat froze mid-lick and watched her cross the room with an expression that seemed to say, 'Are you doing anything that warrants interrupting my bath?'

Stephanie shook her head at the feline. "Sorry. You've had your dinner, now it's my turn."

Coco gave her a disgruntled look and resumed her ablutions.

"You really are an ungrateful beast," Stephanie informed the cat as she rinsed out the tuna can and put it in recycling. "If it wasn't for me, you likely wouldn't even know what tuna tasted like."

Coco had been rescued, soaking wet and half starved, from the backyard in the middle of winter. Stephanie had had no intention of keeping her. She'd planned to warm the cat up, feed it and then make a stop at the local animal shelter the next day. Coco, however, had had other plans. In the morning, the cunning creature had hid under the bed and Stephanie had been forced to leave for work with the cat still in the house.

That night, when she came home determined to rid herself of her unwanted guest, the cat had greeted her at the door, rubbing against her legs and rolling over for a belly rub. After years of coming home to an empty house, Stephanie found herself intrigued with the idea of some companionship and had made one of her rare impulsive decisions. She was going to give the cat a trial run. Now, six months later, she couldn't imagine not having the animal about. It was nice to have a family again, even if it only consisted of one four-footed member.

Coco finished her bath, walked by Stephanie and flicked her tail as if to say, 'I'm off for my nap now. Please don't disturb me.'

The cat seemed to know when it was salad night and never stayed around to beg for tidbits while the meal was being made. Briefly, Stephanie wondered if it was a good thing or not that her life was so predictable that even a cat could follow the pattern. Giving a shrug, she decided that it didn't matter. It was unexciting, but stable, and stable was nothing to sneeze at.

Stephanie's parents had died when she was ten. With no living relatives to take her in, and too old for most couples to consider adopting, she'd ended up in foster care being shuffled from family to family. Already quiet and in shock from her parents' deaths, she'd become more withdrawn and more wary of forming attachments with each new move. She'd also learned to dread change and the uncertainty that came with it. Every house was different; the rules were different, what was acceptable was different. Eventually, she'd become an expert at hiding her real thoughts and feelings, having found that being a quiet observer was the best way to stay out of trouble. Finally, at age fourteen, Mrs. McCreedy had taken her in.

"Welcome, child. Just follow me. I've got a room all set up for you. Set your bags in the corner and I'll give you a tour and then we'll have a nice chat." Mrs. McCreedy had immediately set about making Steph feel as if she belonged.

Mrs. McCreedy was one of those people who never seemed to age. With her grey hair and trademark housedress, the woman had boundless energy, the patience of Job and a wealth of wisdom that she was willing to bestow on anyone who wanted to listen.

She was a career foster parent with a rambling old house that always seemed to have room for one more. Dozens of children had passed through her doors over the years and there was very little that fazed the older woman who listened to Big Band music, but was also as likely to break into her own strange version of rap when the occasion called for it. The whole house would be in hysterics when Mrs. McCreedy decided to cut loose.

Stephanie had stayed with her until she became of legal age. The woman was as close to a mother as she'd had in years, and her time there had been a welcome respite from the insecurity of constantly changing houses. Under her roof, Stephanie had finally started to relax and open up, realizing that she'd finally found a place to call 'home.' Even after all these years Stephanie still kept in contact with Ella, as the woman had asked to be called.

"Mrs. McCreedy is too formal, and Momma McCreedy is too much of a mouthful to say, and anyways, I ain't your momma, but I'll be your friend. I'll care for you and keep you on the right path. You follow the rules, show respect and we gonna get along just fine."

Even now, Stephanie could hear the woman's voice in her head. Every new kid at Mrs. McCreedy's got the same speech and almost all thrived under her roof. Stephanie only knew of one teen that Ella hadn't been able to reach. Jarrod Simpson had come with an attitude that no one had been able to deal with. He'd repeatedly broken curfew, skipped school and disregarded all house rules. The boy had only stayed for three months, but in that short time he'd made Stephanie's life a misery.

Stephanie scowled at the memories Jarrod Simpson brought to mind and tried to lock them firmly away. He'd made her life a misery once before and she wasn't going to let him taint what she had now. Tuesday was *her* night. No negative thoughts allowed!

She got back to work on her salad.

Predictable or not, she had to counteract the effects of her favourite chips and dip, and a salad was the perfect solution. Shredding the lettuce, she added some veggies and topped it off with a low-cal dressing. With the ease of familiarity, she carried her bowl into the living room, flicking on the evening news as she passed by the TV set and then sat down on the sofa. Propping her feet up on the coffee table, she proceeded to munch away while watching the events of the day unfold.

The news anchor cheerfully announced that the hot spell was going to last the rest of the week, a rash of break and enters were plaguing the town, and property taxes were predicted to rise. The depressing news made Stephanie feel even more justified in indulging in her favourite snack. After all, when doom and gloom surrounded you, a little comfort food always made the world seem less bleak.

When her salad was gone and the news finished, she turned off the TV, placed her dishes in the sink, then grabbed the bag of chips while flipping the lid off the dip. She set them on the coffee table within arm's reach, and headed back to the kitchen for something to drink. Her hand hovered over a can of root beer, but then she grabbed a glass of water instead. Much healthier, she told herself, not daring to think of the fat content listed on the container of sour cream and onion dip.

Perusing the books she'd taken out of the library, she chose one with a particularly appealing man on the front cover. Gently shoving Coco to the far end of the sofa, she settled back against the cushions. With a sigh of anticipation, she grabbed a chip and carefully scooped up some dip with it.

Salt and fat, the perfect snack food.

She bit into the crispy treat, enjoying the crunching sound and savouring the taste that spread through her mouth. With the tip of her tongue, she licked her lips gathering in the salty crumbs.

What more could she possibly want out of life than good snacks, a novel to read and a cat at her feet? Wiping her fingers on a napkin, she picked up her book, opened the cover and escaped into the life of a fictitious heroine.

Unfortunately, the heroine's life was almost parallel to her own. Boringly ordinary except for her younger life which was fraught with tragedy. Soon Stephanie found herself recalling her own younger years once again…

Jarrod Simpson arrived at Mrs. McCreedy's early one Saturday morning. His expression was sullen, and even Ella's amiable greeting didn't bring the hint of a smile to his face. Steph peeked at him from where she was curled up in her favourite living room chair reading a book. She'd been going to give him a friendly wave, but something about his cold stare made her duck her head again and rethink the gesture.

Ella was explaining the house rules to Jarrod; curfew, chores, homework, respect. It was the same lecture everyone was given when they arrived. Steph dared another glance in Jarrod's direction and immediately wished she hadn't. He was making no effort to even pretend to listen to his new foster mother. Instead, he was still studying Steph, dragging his gaze the length of her legs. She tugged down the hem of her shorts, wishing she was wearing something that covered more of her. The way Jarrod was looking at her made her feel dirty. Quietly, she slipped from her seat and hurried out of the room. As she left, she could still feel him watching her.

By supper that night, Jarrod was already making sly digs which, over the next few weeks, escalated into persistent taunting, then stealing her lunch money and ripping up her homework. He was an expert at keeping his bullying under the radar though. No one was ever around to witness his behaviour.

Not wanting to cause trouble, Stephanie tried ignoring him, taking pains to never be alone with the boy, but Jarrod always sought her out. In fact, her lack of response seemed to spur him on, and his rude comments took on more threatening undertones. When she came out of the shower, he was always standing outside the bathroom, commenting on her scrawny legs and lack of a figure.

"Ever been kissed?" He sniggered when she blushed. "You got nothing for a man to grab onto," he taunted.

When she tried to walk away, he blocked her path and leered at her, stepping closer until she was pressed back against the wall. She wrapped her arms around her waist as she held her robe closed. The terrycloth material seemed a great deal thinner with Jarrod leering at her. Swallowing hard, she tried to keep her voice steady when she spoke. "Let me pass, please."

"I should show you what it's all about. No other guy will ever want to." Jarrod caged her in on one side with his arm.

Her stomach clenched in fear and her skin crawled. Gathering her courage, she quickly ducked to the side and slipped under his arm, cringing as she brushed against him.

After that, she started wedging a chair under the handle of her bedroom door and during the day she tried even harder to become invisible, standing quietly in the shadows, slipping out of rooms whenever he entered. The large house suddenly seemed much smaller. She thought of telling someone, complaining to Ella, but even as the idea came to mind, Jarrod was there seeming to know what she thinking.

"You cause trouble for me, and I'll make you sorry." Jarrod hissed the warning at her as they passed in the kitchen, grabbing her arm and squeezing hard.

She glanced around but, as usual, no one was looking. Ella was humming a tune, her back turned as she washed dishes. Several others had their heads bent over books as they completed homework at the large kitchen table.

Steph nodded and Jarrod let go. She rubbed her arm and headed to her room having no doubt Jarrod would carry out his threat. Too concerned with all the possible ways he could make her pay, she left her homework books closed and curled up on her bed, staring fearfully at the door.

Eventually, someone noticed what was going on. Her usually good grades began to suffer, she couldn't concentrate in class and a concerned teacher sent her to see the school counsellor. The woman's kind, caring manner caused Stephanie to break into tears, sharing the worries she'd carried the past few months. It had felt good to unburden herself but, unfortunately, the counsellor's next move was to inform Ella.

That night, Jarrod broke into her bedroom, furious at her for getting him in trouble. Ella had given him a tongue lashing and Social Services was coming in the morning.

"You bitch! This is all your fault." He grabbed her wrist and pulled her out of bed. She struggled and he slapped her face. "Why didn't you keep your fucking mouth shut?" He hit her again and a ringing sound filled her ears.

"No! Let me go!" She tried getting away, kicking and hitting, more scared than she'd ever imagined was possible.

"Shit! You'll pay for that!" One of her blows must have hurt him, for Jarrod swore and shoved her away.

She stumbled, falling heavily to her knees. When she tried to crawl away he grabbed her hair and dragged her back. A kick to the stomach had her curling up in pain while a punch to the head left her dazed.

Hurting and frightened, she didn't have any strength left to fight when he pinned her to the floor. "Stupid bitch. Only good for one thing." He kissed her roughly, his lips crushing hers against her teeth, the taste of her own blood seeping into her mouth. She felt she was suffocating as his weight pressed down on her. His hands pulled at her clothing, ripping her top, touching her bare skin.

She managed to bite his lip and scream for help. After that, everything dissolved into confusion.

With a start, Steph realized her hands were clenched tightly on the book in her hand, her muscles tight. With an effort, she forced herself to relax. The attack had been years ago. The police had taken Jarrod away. She'd gone to counselling. It was all in the past.

Dusk was settling and the room had grown dark. She stood and turned on a light then stretched and looked out the window. The street was quiet, a few neighbours already had their lights on. Nothing exciting was happening, which was good. Excitement often meant trouble.

A shiver passed over her. Jarrod had been trouble. She wondered what had ever become of him. She'd never been asked to testify against him. Perhaps because she'd been a minor or maybe he'd had previous offences…? It didn't matter. He was her past and she avoided thinking about it as much as possible.

She drew the curtains and then studied at the book she'd been reading. It had looked so appealing when she'd picked it up in the library, but it was leading her down memory paths she didn't want to travel. Stupid book. The sexy hunk on the front cover had caused her to ignore the blurb on the back. If she'd read that first she'd never have brought the book home. You'd think she'd know by her age not to let a pretty face or a set of toned abs lead her astray!

Chapter 3

He sat outside her home watching her move about inside the house. The living room's large plate glass window provided an excellent view of her coming and going. She carried her snack over to the sofa, and was now moving the cat. He saw the book in her hand and wondered what she was reading tonight. If he knew, he could find a copy for himself and read it along with her. It wasn't much, and she'd never know, but it would give him the impression of being part of her life, of them sharing something together. Maybe tomorrow, while she was at work, he'd slip into her house and find out the title.

No, he admonished himself. Enough snooping; she'll become suspicious if you know too much. He knew the voice of reason was telling the truth, but he was becoming impatient. It had been so long since he'd held her, felt her body pressed against his, seen her eyes flash at him, her stubborn chin rising when he pushed the boundaries too far.

Chuckling, he recalled her temper. For someone who claimed to be so meek and shy, she could certainly lash out when provoked and he loved pushing her buttons just to see the fire rising within her. His Stephanie had hidden depths, depths she didn't even know about. Depths he would have to teach her about.

He hoped she could accept him as her destiny. She was meant for him, as he was for her. That was all that mattered.

It was getting darker now. Through the window, he could see her stand, turn on a lamp and stretch. Her figure was highlighted by the interior lighting and he hungrily ran his gaze over her body. The pink tank top she wore clung to her like a second skin and he easily determined she was braless. His palms itched to cup her breasts, to feel the warm weight and smooth skin. He imagined running his thumb over her nipples and watching them peak. They'd feel stiff against his tongue.

As if sensing his thoughts, she wrapped her arms around her chest and stared out the window. He knew she couldn't possibly see him, but slid lower in his vehicle, just in case. She turned and began to draw the drapes. He sighed. It was a sensible thing for her to do, but it effectively ended his surveillance. It was time to go home. Reluctantly, he started his vehicle and began to drive.

The town was settling for the night. Street lights were just coming on and people who had been out walking were heading into their homes. Crickets were beginning to chirp and an occasional bat could already be seen swooping through the sky in search of an evening meal. Soon all would be quiet.

He loved the night time. The darkness hid his surroundings and he could imagine himself to be anywhere: In the Egyptian desert, by the sea in Scotland or on a mountain in Switzerland. He'd been to all of those places and many more as well. Each had their own distinct characteristics, but at night, in the darkness, there was sameness as well. The stars lighting the sky, the phases of the moon, the sound of his breathing, the feel of his heart beating...

Those were also the times that he was most aware of his own earthly existence; realizing that he lived inside a shell of flesh which allowed him to see and hear and feel, yet which also kept him separate. He was a solitary unit, surrounded by other solitary units, each striving to connect with another, yet never able to fully experience that sense of oneness, of being part of the life energy of someone else.

At night, he could look up at the stars and open himself to the vastness of the universe, allowing his spirit to drift and expand, uniting with the pulse of life that tingled through the darkened sky. It was both an exciting, yet dangerously seductive experience that lured him to leave this earthly existence behind.

His life had been varied; full of passion and power, heights of ecstasy and depths of sorrow, exhilarating experiences punctuating the years of tedium, of waiting. There had been times when he wondered if he'd be able to bear the loneliness and solitude. Times when he'd wondered if he should end his charade and move on to another plane. But then he'd think of her, and know that he had to continue.

He arrived at his apartment building and parked in his assigned spot. When he'd come to Weston three months earlier, he briefly considered purchasing a home. Money was no object. Over the years, he'd amassed a sizeable sum, all carefully hidden away from those who would become too curious about his lifestyle and how he supported it. Yet the effort of buying furnishings and decorating, when his stay would be so short, had seemed pointless. Once he had Stephanie... Well, then he'd see if a house was suitable for his purpose. Instead, he'd temporarily moved into an upscale unit that was already furnished. His few boxes of possessions had mostly remained unpacked in the closet, only the essentials seeing the light of day.

Exiting the car, he walked up to the building. The sound of his shoes clicking on the cement seemed loud in the quiet surroundings. A pool of light spilled from the doorway, welcoming him home. He stepped into the brightness allowing his face to be seen.

"Good evening, Mr. St. Clair." The doorman nodded in recognition and let him in.

"Thank you, Thomas. Beautiful night isn't it?" He responded politely, having long ago recognized the benefits of staying on friendly terms with those who provided you a service.

"Not bad. A trifle warm though."

"Just a bit, but the heat doesn't really bother me."

"You're a lucky one, sir."

"Possibly. Have a good evening, Thomas."

"Thank you, sir. You, too."

After crossing the lobby, he entered the elevator and headed to the sixth floor. Thankfully, no one else got on and he made it to his apartment without having to engage in any more small talk. It wasn't that he disliked people, but rather he was so fixated on Stephanie right now, it irritated to have others interrupting his thoughts. Once he finally had her, his usual sociable nature would reappear.

He entered his apartment and shut the door. For a moment, he stood in the darkness, taking in the silence. After all these years, he should be used to it, but it never became easier; the emptiness, the sterility, the loneliness.

His Stephanie wasn't here.

Shedding his T-shirt, he walked out onto the balcony. Resting his forearms against the railing, he gazed over the town. Several miles away, Stephanie was probably still lying on her couch, reading. He wondered if the chips and dip were gone yet. His stomach growled, reminding him that he hadn't eaten yet today, except for a granola bar and a can of cola. He'd better find something to keep this body fuelled. If he was sick or weak, he wouldn't be able to enjoy being with her.

Food didn't interest him, yet he forced himself to find a frozen dinner and place it in the microwave. Leaning against the counter, he waited for it to cook. He'd eat, go to bed and hopefully sleep through the night.

Sleep had been evasive of late—all Stephanie's fault, he ruefully acknowledged. Thoughts of her consumed him and he was restless, unable to settle. Would he be able to stay in bed tonight, or would he find himself driving by her house at three in the morning as he had so often these past weeks?

It had been easier when he first came to town. He'd finally located her and knew he had to spend time researching her life, discovering what had happened to her since they'd last met. But now, the background work was over. The time for action was upon him and anticipation was playing hell with his sleep, his appetite, his nerves...

It had to be this week. If he waited any longer, he'd surely lose all self-control and that would never do.

The microwave dinged, signalling that his food was ready. He sat down to eat, grabbing the daily paper from the counter where he'd tossed it that morning. The headlines proclaimed that a rash of break and enters were sweeping Weston. So far, no one had been injured and the police had few leads except that the perpetrator was probably a male. A strand of dark hair had been found, caught in the window casing at one of the crime scenes, and DNA testing would be done with the hope of finding a match in the database.

There won't be a match, he thought as he eyed a forkful of vegetables. The police were always hopeful, but there never was. Carefully, he plucked a piece of his own hair from the food and let the dark strand fall to the floor before resuming his meal.

~~~

That night, Stephanie awoke around three-thirty, hot and sweaty and cursing the broken air conditioner. The T-shirt she slept in stuck to her damp skin and the sheets were tangled around her legs. Finger combing her hair away from her face, she furrowed her brow as remnants of her erotic dream ran through her mind. She'd been in France—though how she knew that, she was unsure—and a man had been with her, caressing her and whispering in her ear in a language she didn't understand. His bare skin had been hot under her hands and she could feel his muscles shifting as he moved over her, kissing her deeply while he parted her legs with his knee... And then she'd jerked awake, her body aching in frustration.

Ruefully, she laughed at herself. Such a scenario would never happen in her real life, but lately her subconscious was obviously trying to make up for her sterile existence, forcing her dreams to become increasingly steamier and more sensual each night. It could be the combined result of her bedtime reading material and the hot weather, she speculated, while untangling herself from the sheets. Whatever the cause, once again she was up in the middle of the night.

She made her way to the bathroom and, after doing what was needed, wandered into the kitchen in search of a glass of cold water. Finding money in the budget to repair the broken air conditioning unit would have to become a priority, she decided. The heat this summer was ridiculous, and she was losing far too much sleep. Setting the glass in the sink, she padded back to the bedroom, but veered off course when she heard Coco meowing loudly in the living room.

The beast as perched on the window ledge, only its rear end visible, the front half hidden by the curtain it had burrowed under.
~~~

"What's the matter, sweetie?" She scratched the cat's ears and, parting the curtain, peered outside, trying to see what had captured her pet's attention. Coco was staring fixedly down the street. It seemed quiet. Darkened houses lined the silent street with puddles of light from the lamp posts creating a hop-scotch pattern down the road. Stephanie squinted and noticed a dark-coloured car pulled up by the curb a few houses down. It was situated between the pools of light and difficult to see. Was there someone in it? She couldn't be sure.

A strange feeling washed over her. It was anticipation mixed with fear, and a sense of a memory, or an awareness, trying to push its way into her consciousness. She frowned and tried to bring it into focus, but as was so often the case, the harder she tried, the more elusive it became until it slipped away completely.

Frowning, she looked at the car again. "That's unusual," she muttered to the cat. "Who would be out at this time of night?"

She stood in her darkened window for a few more minutes, watching and waiting, though she wasn't sure why. Finally, she gave herself a shake. It was nonsense to spend the night standing by the window when she had to be up for work in just a few hours. Picking up the feline, she twitched the curtains back into place before wandering back to her bedroom.

"It's probably just someone like me who couldn't sleep because of the heat and decided to take a drive." She informed Coco of her conclusion before setting the beast down on the floor.

She straightened the tangled sheets and propped the fan in the window. With any luck, she might be able to draw some cooler night air into the stuffy room.

Crawling back into bed, she fluffed her pillow and closed her eyes, soon lost once again in a restless dream world filled with strange locations, ghostly images and someone incessantly calling her name.

Chapter 4

Thursday morning Stephanie arrived at her store, 'Fields of Flowers', only minutes before opening time. She'd had to leave work early the previous day to be home when the repairman came to look at her air conditioner. Deciding she'd spent too many sleepless nights suffering from the heat, she had finally broken down and called to see about having the unit fixed. The repair man had charged her an exorbitant amount just to look at the machine, only to announce that it would cost more to fix it than it was worth and she should buy a new one. That, of course, was out of the question. The small savings that she had would never cover the amount needed. She'd just have to make do with open windows and a fan this year.

As a result of that bit of bad news, she'd spent an uneasy night tossing and turning in bed and groggily awoke to the annoying sound of her alarm ringing in her ear. A shower had done little to improve her mood and then Coco had slipped out of the house when she'd reached for the newspaper. She'd spent at least a half an hour trying to catch the elusive creature before resorting to opening a can of tuna in order to entice the annoying beast into the kitchen. Some people would have just let the cat stay outside for the day, but Stephanie worried that the animal might wander off and not return. After being alone for so long, the thought of losing her only companion was decidedly unpalatable. Once she'd caught the cat, she'd had to hurry to get ready for work and now she was late.

Being the owner meant she had certain privileges and arriving late was one of them. However, Stephanie felt guilty about leaving Paula to do all of the opening up chores on her own, especially when she'd left the woman to close up the night before. As she rushed in, Paula looked up from behind the counter and smiled.

"Late are we? Now let me guess. You had a date with a dashingly handsome man and spent the night making wild passionate love until you were exhausted. Then you had to tear yourself out of his arms this morning in order to get ready. Am I right?"

Stephanie rolled her eyes and shook her head. Paula was an unrepentant romantic who couldn't understand why her boss wasn't out trawling for men every night. "No, not even close. Coco slipped out and I had to resort to opening up a can of tuna to get her to come back inside."

"That cat has you trained. Isn't this the third time that's happened?"

"Fourth, actually, but who's counting?" Stephanie stored her purse in the small office at the back of the shop and pinned on her name tag, which proclaimed her to be Stephanie Fields, Owner. She still got a slight thrill every time she read the little brass tag with flowers engraved in one corner. Her parents had left her a small inheritance, which she'd received when she turned twenty-one. Some good investments had provided her with a tidy nest egg, and, when the store had come up for sale, she'd used the money as a down payment. That was three years ago and at the age of twenty-seven she was the proud proprietress of her own business. Of course, the bank still owned over half, but that was a minor detail. The flower shop was slowly building a clientele, and she made sufficient profit that she was able to pay the mortgage each month and Paula's wages. Her living expenses had to be kept to the bare minimum, but that was fine. She had a roof over her head—also mortgaged—and food. Beyond that, her needs were few.

"What still needs to be done?" She turned over the 'Open' sign in the front window before looking back inquiringly at Paula.

"Not much. I've refreshed the pre-made bouquets and checked that the flowers all have fresh water. Petty cash is in the till, and the orders that have to be filled today are on the counter."

"You're so darn efficient; I guess I could have just stayed home this morning then, right?"

"Don't even think about it!" Paula began to flick through the list of work orders that were sitting on the desk. "We have that shipment of flowers coming in for the Johnston wedding and all those bridesmaid bouquets to work on. The Chamber of Commerce needs centrepieces made up for the Friday luncheon, we have three birthday deliveries all in different parts of town and," she set down the papers and looked at Stephanie, "did you read in the paper that Ben Miller died? There'll be tons of orders coming in for funeral arrangements."

"Okay, okay." Stephanie threw her hands up in mock horror. "I didn't mean it. Don't tell me anymore. I'm exhausted just listening to you."

Paula laughed and leaned her hip against the counter. "So how did it go with the repairman? Was he single? Good looking?"

"No. He was old enough to be my father and he had a receding hairline. He also charged me forty dollars to look at the air conditioner only to tell me it was too old to fix."

"Bummer. What are you going to do?"

"Nothing. Sweat a lot. Maybe buy another fan. A new air conditioner is out of the question this year." Stephanie grabbed a tissue as she felt a sneeze coming on and changed to an equally depressing topic. "I don't know, Paula. These allergy pills the doctor gave me don't seem to be doing a lot of good." She punctuated her comment with three vigorous sneezes. "He thinks I'm allergic to Coco, but I'm sneezing and sniffling at work, too."

"Maybe you're allergic to flowers."

"Don't even think that!"

"I'm just teasing." Paula moved to adjust a display of carnations. "You've worked here for years without a problem and you've had Coco for what? Six months now? And you suddenly develop an allergy? Maybe it's just a summer cold that won't go away."

"Perhaps. I suppose if I actually remembered to take the pills more often it might help, too. But they make me feel sort of strange—foggy and nervous, even a bit paranoid that someone's watching me. And I have the weirdest dreams..."

She let her voice trail off, not sure if she wanted to reveal the actual content.

"Do they involve handsome, sexy men?" Paula asked eagerly.

Stephanie glared at her friend hoping her face wasn't turning red. Paula's comment had hit a bit too close to home. Thankfully the phone rang and the conversation was dropped as the two friends got to work, their social time finished.

As predicted, it was a busy day. Stephanie was on her feet all morning and her back ached from leaning over the worktable. With customers constantly in and out, she'd taken no time for lunch, instead asking Paula to bring back a coffee and a toasted bagel when she returned from making deliveries. It was now after two o'clock and the coffee was sitting untouched on the counter while the bagel, cold and tough, had only one bite out of it.

Smiling politely, she finished wrapping tissue around a single rosebud with an accent of some baby's breath and ferns. "Here you go, sir. I hope your wife enjoys this."

The man had a dour expression on his face and had been studying the store quite intently, almost as if he wanted to buy the place, but found it lacking on several key points. Stephanie wondered what he was thinking. It made her feel odd, as if she and her establishment were under a microscope.

'Maybe he's having a bad day and is just out of sorts,' she thought to herself. He was handing her some bills just as the phone rang. Taking his money and picking up the receiver at the same time, she smiled apologetically at him. "Fields of Flowers, could you hold for a minute please?"

Quickly giving the man his change, she wished him a nice day. After staring suspiciously at the till, his change and then her, he turned and left. She was pleased to see him leave. He'd made her uncomfortable and she felt sorry for his wife. The flashing light on the phone reminded her that she had a customer waiting on hold. Pushing the incident from her mind, she ignored the growl in her stomach and picked up the phone, politely thanking whoever was on the other end for waiting.

Gazing longingly at her bagel, she took down the particulars for more funeral arrangements for the late Mr. Miller. He'd been a well-known and liked figure in the community, so the number of orders wasn't really surprising. As she jotted the information on her notepad, the jingling of the bell attached to the front door signalled the arrival of yet another customer and she briefly wished the business wasn't doing quite so well at present. Paula was swamped in the back, trying to keep up with the requests that were pouring in, and Stephanie had said she'd manage the front by herself. At the moment however, she was questioning the wisdom of that decision.

All she could see of this newest customer was the back of a dark head set on broad shoulders. He seemed to be busy examining the pre-arranged displays and she inwardly smiled in relief. It was always a bit of a chance, having things pre-made because possibly no one would buy them, but on the other hand, they were a time saver on days like this.

Focusing her attention back on the caller, she repeated the order, confirmed the address, method of payment and the message to be written on the card. "Okay, we'll have that sent out. Thank you for choosing Fields of Flowers."

Stephanie hung up the phone and looked at the new customer again. He still appeared to be absorbed in the display, so she quickly turned her back and grabbed a bite of bagel, chewing as quickly as possible. She was just reaching for her cold coffee to wash it down with, when someone spoke behind her.

"Excuse me. Could you—"

She gave a start and knocked the cup over. Brown liquid quickly spread over the countertop.

"Oh no!" She grabbed for the cup and righted it, then picked up the bagel and shook the coffee off of it while simultaneously smiling over her shoulder at the gentleman standing behind her. "Sorry! I'll be right with you... I just need to clean this up."

The coffee spill was rapidly drifting towards the little stack of cards and envelopes sitting on the counter. Stephanie dropped her bagel in favour of saving the tags. The bagel bounced off the counter and landed on the floor, buttered side down, right in front of the customer's feet.

"Damn!" She whispered under her breath.

"Let me help," the man offered, flashing a smile her way. He grabbed some paper towels from the shelf behind her, his arm brushing against hers as he reached across. The faintly spicy scent of his cologne drifted past and Stephanie's mind registered it as pleasantly inviting.

"No! That's all right. I can do it." Even as she protested, he was blotting up the coffee. Stephanie set the stack of cards and envelopes down in a safe location, and moved the almost empty coffee cup out of harm's way.

"It's no problem. It's my fault anyway for startling you." He efficiently wiped up the mess, dropped the wet paper towels in the garbage and picked up the bagel off of the floor. "Yours?" he asked with raised brows. His blue eyes met hers and she felt an unexpected jolt of recognition. Confused, she immediately looked away. If she didn't know better, she'd say that she had met him before; something about his eyes seemed strangely familiar.

"Uh, yeah. It was my lunch, but I think it's passed its prime now." She took the bagel from him and deposited it in the garbage, carefully avoiding his gaze.

"Your lunch? At two-thirty?"

"It's been a busy day." She offered by way of an explanation, shrugging and looking slightly to the left of his shoulder rather than directly at him. Something about this man made her nervous... Or was it excitement? She wasn't sure what to call it, but the feeling was unfamiliar. Pasting on her professional facade, she addressed him. "How may I help you?"

"I was wondering how much you charge for a dozen daisies."

"Daisies? Not roses?" She darted a glance at him and found that he was staring at her, a faint trace of amusement evident on his lips.

"That's right. She's partial to daisies."

"So am I." Stephanie smiled and reached for the order pad. "Gerber daisies or—"

"Just plain white Shastas." He answered before she could even finish the question.

"With a vase or without?"

"I'm sure she has lots of vases already."

Stephanie nodded, busily writing down the particulars. "Delivered or would you be picking them up?"

"I'm not sure."

"Oh... Well when would you want them by?"

"I'm not sure of that either."

She looked up at him and raised her eyebrows.

He grinned sheepishly. "I haven't asked her out yet, so I don't know if it will be today or tomorrow."

Stephanie set the pen down and tried to hide her exasperation. It had been a busy day. Her lunch—such as it was—was now in the garbage. She didn't feel like playing games. "Well, when you find out, let me know and I'll give you a price. There's a five percent discount on pre-orders of more than two days."

"Good to know." He nodded. "So, will you go out to dinner with me?"

"I beg your pardon?" His sudden change of topic had her staring at him in confusion.

"Will you go out to dinner with me? I need to know so I can order the daisies." He gave her a wide friendly smile, the corners of his eyes crinkling slightly.

"You want to go out to dinner? With me?" Even though she knew she was repeating his question and probably sounded like an idiot, she wanted clarification. Strange men didn't just walk up to her and ask her out every day.

"I caused you to ruin your lunch. It's the least I can do." He leaned casually against the counter, watching her reaction and patiently waiting for her answer.

"Oh, no. That's not necessary. It was mostly my fault." She knew she was stumbling over her words. It was a sympathy date; she could understand that. He felt sorry for her, and slightly responsible for her lost lunch. She'd reassure him. He'd feel he'd done his duty, and be on his way taking with him the strange feeling that was coming to life inside her. "The coffee was cold and the bagel was a bit stale anyway."

"I'd still like to make it up to you."

"But it was only a bagel!" His insistence was making her feel almost panicky. Men didn't go out of their way to make a date with her! She'd given him an out. Why wasn't he taking it?

"Well, would it make you feel better if I took you out for coffee and a bagel then? You know the old saying: An eye for an eye, a bagel for a bagel."

Despite herself she laughed and actually looked at him, her earlier wariness temporarily pushed aside. "It would make more sense. But I really can't—"

"Of course you can, Stephanie!" Paula suddenly appeared from the backroom, where no doubt she'd been observing the whole incident. "I'll watch the store. You go and eat."

"But—" Stephanie sputtered in protest.

Paula smiled at the man. "Just a minute." She grabbed Stephanie's arm and yanked her a few feet over to the display of stuffed animals and balloons that could be purchased to go with floral arrangements. She spoke in hushed but insistent tones. "Stephanie, I know you're cautious and I know why. I respect your feelings. But this is just a bagel in a public restaurant, with lots of other people around. There's no need to worry. Besides, he's gorgeous!"

"But—"

"No more buts. If you don't eat, you get grumpy and I don't want a grumpy boss. Now go!" She took Stephanie by the shoulders, gave her a half turn, and pushed her towards the door. "She's ready." Paula called to the man who was watching the interaction between the two of them with obvious interest.

Out of the corner of her eye, Stephanie noticed her friend winking at the dark haired man. She opened her mouth to protest, but found herself being gently propelled out the door and down the sidewalk.

"What was that all about?" She looked at her companion suspiciously.

"What was what about?"

"Paula winked at you!"

"Really? Maybe she had something in her eye." He opened the door to the donut shop that was just three doors down from Fields of Flowers. It was a small establishment patronized by those who worked in the area. The décor was older, but it was clean and the coffee always fresh. Stephanie entered and allowed herself to be led up to the counter.

"Hey Steph!" The server gave her a wide smile. "The usual? Medium coffee, two creams, two sugars and a toasted cinnamon raisin bagel with butter?" Mandy Smyth was working behind the counter today. She was in high school and lived across the street and two doors down from Stephanie's home.

Stephanie nodded while holding back a sigh. Her life was so lacking in spontaneity. What would happen if she ever did something really crazy like—gasp—ordering a sesame seed bagel with cream cheese? Would the world be able to stand the shock?

The gentleman beside her gave no visible reaction to the fact that her order was boringly predictable. Instead, he added his own request. "And I'll have a large, black."

"Sure." Mandy's eyes darted from Stephanie to the man beside her and smiled before filling their order.

Stephanie groaned inwardly. Mandy was a nice kid, but she loved to gossip. Now everyone would know she was having coffee with someone. Well, there was nothing she could do about it. Resigned to her fate, she listened as the young server chatted away while preparing their order.

"Did you hear about the robbery on our street last night? It was three doors down from your place." Mandy spoke over her shoulder as she popped a bagel in the toaster. "Police say the guy broke in while Mr. and Mrs. Thompson were sleeping. He took their jewellery, that new laptop their kids bought him for his birthday and all the money that Mrs. Thompson keeps in the cookie jar."

"Oh, that's awful! Were they hurt?" Stephanie frowned. Mr. and Mrs. Thompson were a sweet elderly couple in their early seventies. She'd been over there a few times helping Mr. Thompson learn the intricacies of the World Wide Web and his webcam. Their oldest son had moved to Australia and they were trying to keep in touch using the internet. The poor man would be devastated to have lost his new toy.

"Not that I know of, but police said it was weird how the thief knew right where to look for some of the stuff, like he'd been 'casing the joint' or something." Mandy spoke with excitement and seemed pleased to be able to use some of the jargon she'd picked up from TV. "Sort of scary isn't it, right close to home and all?"

Stephanie nodded in agreement, thinking of the car she'd seen parked down the road just the other night. Perhaps she should tell the police about it, though she didn't know the type of car or even the model. Hmm... Possibly it wasn't a very great clue after all. Well, she'd think about it and in the meantime double check the locks on her house. If the thief had 'cased the joint', as Mandy as had said, he might be looking at the other houses in the neighbourhood as well. She recalled how she'd felt that someone was watching her and wondered if her house was on the list of places to rob. Not that she had anything worth stealing, but still, the idea of someone wandering through her home…

Her train of thought was interrupted by Mandy placing a tray of food in front of her. The dark haired man had listened quietly to their exchange, but hadn't interrupted to ask any questions. Stephanie had almost forgotten he was there. He paid for the food and carried their tray as Stephanie led the way to a table in the corner.

She sat down and took a sip of her coffee, closing her eyes and savouring the feel of the warm, liquid caffeine sliding down her throat. "Thanks. This is very kind of you."

"Kind? Possibly." He shrugged. "I actually see it as self-serving since I get what I wanted, which was to spend some time with you.

Stephanie felt heat flooding her cheeks and she ducked her head, taking a bite of her bagel. She could feel his eyes on her, and after swallowing, she spoke. "I'm Stephanie Fields, by the way."

"I know."

"You do?"

"Name tag." He smiled and nodded towards her lapel. "It's very nice by the way."

She glanced down and felt a bit silly. "Thanks—I'm rather fond of it. You don't have one though, a nametag that is."

"No I don't." He smiled again and she found herself staring at his eyes. They seemed to be full of laughter as if he was enjoying some secret joke. She wondered if she was the source of his amusement and felt herself becoming annoyed with him. Her irritation filtered into her tone of voice.

"Care to share?"

"I'm Jacob St. Clair, Jake to my friends." He grinned, as if pleased with himself for having managed to get under her skin. She took his extended hand, and he held on to hers a second longer than socially acceptable before letting go.

Stephanie put her hand in her lap and wiggled her fingers. They felt strange; tingling where they had touched him. She looked at him speculatively. A wide easy smile made him seem approachable—non-threatening, even—and for some reason her usual wariness seemed to be rapidly melting away.

He had a lean, muscular build with wide shoulders and he must be around six feet tall, since she'd had to look up at him in the store. His hair was dark and thick, an errant lock falling over his forehead. In her opinion, it was a trifle too long at the back and brushed his collar. Altogether, it was a very pleasing appearance—vaguely familiar, though she couldn't place him. It was that darn déjà vu feeling again, she mused. Sometimes she was sure her brain was wired wrong.

Silence had fallen between them and she realized that she'd been studying him intently. Once again his bright blue eyes were looking at her and sparkling with some inner delight. Flustered at having been caught staring, she tried to turn the tables on him.

"So Jacob St. Clair, tell me. Why did you just happen to stop in today and ask about daisies?"

"Please, call me Jake." He took a sip of coffee, and glanced at her over the rim. "Do you believe in fate? Destiny?"

"No." She answered bluntly.

"You should. Fate, destiny—whatever you want to call it—it does happen."

She said nothing and just stared at him.

Finally he shrugged and ducked his head sheepishly. "All right. You have me. I saw you leaving the store the other day and stopped in to ask your assistant about you."

"Oh really?" Steph clenched her fingers tightly around the coffee cup she'd been nursing. "I think I'll have to have a little chat with her when I get back."

"Don't be angry." He reached across the table and gently touched her hand. "She didn't give me anything specific, just that you'd be in today, that you liked daisies and that, to the best of her knowledge, you weren't seeing anyone. No name, no address or phone number."

"Well..." His touch distracted her, her nerve endings quivering from the contact. "I guess I'll only give her a small tongue lashing then."

Jacob smiled at her. "I'm really glad you agreed to come. I feel like our meeting was just meant to be."

Chapter 5

He'd spent a half hour with her, but all too soon she'd gone back to work. At least she'd agreed to see him again, and for that he was thankful. Of course, there really was no doubt—she was meant to be his, but nevertheless, he'd been worried—it was the age-old fear that plagued every man asking a woman for a date. Some things never change, he mused.

Tomorrow night, it was arranged that he'd meet her after work and they'd go to dinner together. It was so typical of her, the way she'd refused to give him her address or phone number. Not that he needed them; they were already committed to his memory. Instead of complaining over her reticence, he'd commended her on being so cautious. In fact, he'd even given her his references so that she could check up on him, if she wished.

He wasn't worried.

After all this time, he was an expert at creating an identity. There were no gaps in his background. Everything would check out and she would accept him as Jacob St. Clair, a financial advisor who had invested wisely and was now considering starting a business in Weston.

Weston was a nice place if you liked a quiet life. The population was around 30,000. Not too small, yet not quite a city. It boasted several up-scale restaurants and stores as well as a plethora of fast food chains and mom and pop diners. There were two shopping malls, a theatre and a six screen cinema complex. People were friendly, but not too nosey. Yes, all in all, it fit the bill. A good place to settle for a while until circumstances forced a change. Once Stephanie was gone...

He pushed the thought from his mind. The inevitable would happen all too soon just as it always did and then he'd have to move on, start over again.

Until that fateful day occurred, however, he would enjoy himself while rediscovering her. She thought she was shy and preferred a quiet, predictable life, but he knew differently. He'd enjoyed pushing her buttons today and watching the irritation grow inside her while she tried to remain calm and polite. There was a spitfire inside her just waiting to be set free. Circumstances in her earlier life had temporarily corralled it, but under his tutelage the spark would come to life. He hoped it wouldn't take too long to gain her trust and get her to open up. Once she believed that his intentions were honourable, things should proceed along nicely, just as he had planned.

He paced across the apartment, unsure of what to do. After weeks of research and tailing her day and night, he'd finally moved beyond that stage and first contact had been made. All he needed to do was wait until six-thirty tomorrow night. It was only twenty-two hours. Surely he could find something to fill his time. The blandly furnished apartment offered little to distract him. A few books lined the shelves behind the couch, but none were to his taste.

Dropping down into the beige recliner, he turned on the television and flipped through the channels. Movies, a sitcom, a baseball game... He finally settled on the news. A report was just coming on about the unusual number of burglaries that had occurred over the past few months. As the newscaster read the specifics of the various break-ins, his mind drifted to the conversation Stephanie had had with the waitress at the donut shop.

Last night there had been a burglary just doors away from Stephanie. It had been the brown house, with the sliding French doors at the back. After all of his time watching her, he was an expert on the area, its occupants and their habits. He knew who lived where, when they were out, even the type of lifestyle they had. Mr. and Mrs. Thompson, the couple who'd been burgled had been perfect targets; an elderly couple who were both hard of hearing and wouldn't notice a bomb going off while they slept.

Next to the Thompsons, was Mr. Hardy, a fifty-something bachelor with a large dog that barked at everyone. Not a good candidate for break and enter at all. The Coulters who lived beside Stephanie really needed to install better doors and windows. The frames fit poorly—they appeared to be the originals the house had been built with—and no doubt only a little bit of effort would have them sliding open with ease.

Stephanie's house had good locks, and her windows were secure except for the fact that she slept with her bedroom window open. In a way it was understandable. Her air conditioner had broken three weeks ago, and she was trying to cool the room down for sleeping. But open windows at night were just inviting trouble.

He turned off the TV and stared around the room looking for inspiration, for something, anything, to do. The walls were beige except for the muted wallpaper that covered one end of the living room. Bland artwork hung on the walls, a few figurines were scattered about the table tops in what was likely a misguided attempt to make the place look homey. Sighing, he gave in to the pull of the night and walked out onto the balcony.

Muffled sounds came from the adjoining apartment but it was easy to ignore them. The neighbours were of no interest to him. But Stephanie… He gripped the railing firmly while staring in the direction of her house. He wouldn't go to her neighbourhood tonight, despite the need that clawed at him. With the break-in, police would be patrolling the area more frequently. It would be too dangerous to watch her tonight. Someone might see him and question why he was sitting in his car, staring at her house.

He rolled his head and shrugged his shoulders, trying to ease the tension that filled his body. Staring up at the darkening night sky, he watched the stars slowly appear, little pin pricks of light against the velvet dome. It was hard to imagine that they were in fact great seething balls of fire, each supporting their own array of planets many light years away.

The heavens were vast, endless, and they called out to him. A feeling of separation slowly came over him, as if he was floating outside himself, not really part of this world anymore, but part of the energy that made up the universe. He was no longer attached to the weaknesses of a human body. Endless possibilities awaited him, if he'd just leave this existence behind.

'There's still time,' the voices in his head whispered to him. *'If you'd only let go, there is still time to really live, to be what you were meant to be. You're better than these frail humans that surround you. Just think of how easily you fool their gullible minds. Why stay bound to their ridiculous rules? You are like a god compared to them...'*

As if in a dream, he hovered over the apartment watching himself cross the room and opening the fridge, taking out a can of pop then returning to the balcony to drink it. What else might he do, while watching himself in this disembodied manner? Where did his control over this body end? If he just left it, would it die or would it function on its own? Did he really want to be confined within such a finite existence when the whole universe awaited him? Maybe…

"No!" He came to himself and felt his knees buckle with the suddenness of his return. Sweat beaded his forehead and his hand trembled, sloshing some of the soda onto his skin. That hadn't happened in ages. Why now? Why were they doing this to him? He'd told them before to leave him alone. He didn't want the voices talking to him, planting ideas in his mind. His thoughts were his own. It was his choice to be here. He looked up and growled at the heavens. "Quit trying to entice me away. I've made my decision. I don't want you in my head. Leave me alone—now!"

The wind stirred and the trees rustled. He listened and watched and felt, using all of his senses to try and determine if they were really gone. All was quiet. He was alone. Nothing touched his mind. He crushed the can in his hand and cursed as the remaining carbonated drink gushed up over the top and onto the floor, little drops splashing up on his legs and feet.

He hated it when the voices took over. They had no right to do that. They knew better, but still they kept coming back, trying to control him...change him. Sometimes they did, briefly, when his guard was down, when he was tired or too emotionally wrought. He'd find himself floating in the night, becoming one with the energy of the universe. He was a god, omnipotent, powerful, free of the constraints of earthly existence.

It was a heady feeling. Addictive. Seductive. It beckoned to him and he fought to turn his back on the temptation that was laid out before him.

Stephanie was the problem, he decided. She was the reason for his weakness. Never had it been this long that he'd been kept away from the one he loved. The need inside him was too great; the yearning to belong, to become one was almost overwhelming. That was why the voices were back; why they were trying to make him do things he didn't want to do. They sensed he was vulnerable.

As he thought of Stephanie, he felt the muscles in his jaw tighten. He breathed deeply trying to control the hunger inside, a hunger only she could quell. The need was raw, almost painful and he desperately searched his mind for something to ease the feeling that was threatening to overtake him. Striding into the bedroom, he pulled open his top dresser drawer and took out a thin accordion file folder. Stephanie's name was printed neatly on the outside.

Walking to the bed, he flipped through the contents, pausing to read some before moving onward. Finally, at the back, he found the collection of pictures and lovingly began to go through them. Her hair and clothing changed, but her eyes were always the same. They seemed to reach out to him, calling to him, asking him: 'Where are you? When will you come for me?

"I'm here, Stephanie. I've finally come for you." He spoke lovingly to one of the photos. "I know it took a while and I'm sorry, but that's behind us now. We're together again, just like we should be, like we were meant to be. Together, for the rest of your life." He gently traced her lovely features then lay back on the bed willing his body to relax. Placing the photos on the pillow beside him, he drifted off to sleep.

Chapter 6

Stephanie sighed in frustration and checked the clock yet again. It was almost six thirty and Jake would be here soon. She was both excited and nervous about the prospect of seeing him again, but wondered what he'd say when she had to break the date.

She'd surprised herself when she'd accepted his invitation—it usually took her a while to warm up to strangers, especially men, but before she'd even realized what was happening, she had made arrangements to see him. Even now, she wasn't sure what he'd said or done that had made her agree. Had it been his smile, his quirky sense of humour, or his gentle teasing? Perhaps it'd been the way he'd looked at her as if she was the most fascinating person he'd ever met, or the confidence in his voice. Whatever it was, something about him had her falling in with his plans despite herself.

But now these floral arrangements had to be done for the Johnston wedding tomorrow, and she hadn't been able to start on them earlier because the delivery truck had been late. Then Paula's three year old daughter had become ill, and the babysitter had called asking her to come and collect the child so Paula had had to leave early. She'd apologized profusely about leaving Stephanie with so much work, but it couldn't be helped.

Stephanie understood. She knew better than most that if you were lucky enough to have a family, they came first, but, still it was...frustrating.

So now she was sitting by herself, on a Friday night, facing over two hours' worth of work. There was no way she'd be done in the next fifteen minutes, and she couldn't ask the man to wait until she was finished. Double checking the bouquet she'd just completed, she set it aside and began working on the next one, her mind preoccupied with thoughts of Jake. He was good looking, friendly and not too pushy; just enough to let her know that he was really interested. His references checked out too. Self-employed, successful, planning on starting a local business... A guy like that didn't come along every day—at least not in her life—and now she'd have to turn him away.

It was strange. She hadn't realized how much she wanted to have someone in her life until yesterday when she'd met Jake. Usually, she felt her life was fine as it was. Her job kept her busy. Coco kept her warm at night. Paula was a good friend and they had a great time together taking her daughter, Chelsea, on outings. Her holidays were spent with Mrs. McCreedy or Paula's family. Finding a man hadn't really figured largely in her plans. Given her past, she assumed she'd spend her life alone, and that was fine.

But now, after spending just a short time with Jake, she felt an emptiness that she hadn't been aware of before and she realized that she wanted it filled. Unfortunately, her chance of filling it was rapidly disappearing with each tick of the clock. Her usually calm, quiet personality was disappearing under a wave of resentment and she jabbed a white rosebud into the floral foam with more force than necessary.

"What did that flower do to you?"

Stephanie jumped and clutched her hand to her chest while turning to find the man she'd just been thinking about standing behind her. "What? Oh... Jake... It's you. Don't do that to me." She closed her eyes and took a deep breath to calm her pounding heart. "I'm sorry. I didn't hear you come in. I was so busy working—"

"That's okay. I'm sorry I startled you." He nodded towards the arrangement she was working on. "So, what did that rosebud do to tick you off?"

"Nothing." She shrugged, adjusting the flower before looking up at the man beside her. "I'm just a little upset. I'm really sorry, but I have to break our date. I need to have all of these bouquets ready for a wedding tomorrow, and everything has gone wrong today." She gave him an apologetic look. "It's a shame that you came all this way for nothing. I would have called, but I didn't have your cell phone number and there was no answer at your home, though I did leave a voice mail."

He frowned, and the look on his face seemed to be genuine disappointment rather than just being peeved at having his evening suddenly free. "I was out and haven't checked my messages yet. I'm sorry to hear that your day went badly. How long will it take you to finish, do you think?"

"If all goes well, two hours, maybe a little longer. Then I still have to cash out and clean up... I can't ask you to wait that long."

"Is there anything I could do to help?"

"No, not really, but thanks for asking." She smiled regretfully while thinking how nice it was of him to offer. Not many men would be willing to hang around a flower shop late at night.

"Stephanie, I really want us to spend some time together. I don't mind waiting. Even if we just go for a burger and fries it would be fine." He stared at her intently and Stephanie felt his gaze reaching out to her, drawing her in, willing her to agree.

"I suppose..." She was surprised to find that she was standing close enough to him that she could feel the heat radiating from his body. Her hands were clasped in his; she didn't even remember that happening.

"Great." He gave her hands a gentle squeeze. "I've got some errands I can run and I'll be back in a couple of hours. If you're not ready, I'll just wait, okay?"

"Sure. It's really nice of you to be so understanding."

Jake squeezed her hands gently again, then reached out and ran the back of his hand down her cheek and traced his thumb across her lips. "I've been looking forward to this all day. I'll see you soon," he whispered before quietly walking out the door.

As the door shut behind him, Stephanie touched her face where his hand had been. Her skin felt warm and her lips tingled. "Oh boy, I've got it bad for him already."

After completing the floral arrangements in record time, she took off her work apron and draped it over her desk chair. She grabbed the broom and began sweeping up the leaves and stray floral foam, humming softly to herself as she anticipated Jake's arrival. A sound at the rear door had her looking up, a smile starting to form on her lips. At first she thought it was Jake and wondered why he was coming to the back door, but then decided he'd probably seen the "closed" sign and the darkened front window and had thought she'd be using the rear entrance. Actually, the back door was only opened for deliveries, but he wouldn't know that.

She leant her broom against the counter and took a few steps towards the door, but then stopped as a cold feeling swept over her. The doorknob was turning very slowly to the left, and then the right like someone was testing it, but trying not to make any noise. There'd been no knock—surely Jake would knock and not just walk straight in, right? Instead there was a faint scraping sound of metal on metal, almost as if the lock was being picked.

Stephanie stared at the door transfixed. Her heart was pounding in her chest as she recalled the rash of break-ins around the town. She grabbed onto the table to steady herself as she felt her legs tremble. Oh God, someone was breaking in, and she was here by herself!

Keeping her eyes fixed on the door knob, she began to retreat, bending and fumbling for her purse then quietly backing out into the front display room. As the curtain fell shut, blocking her view of the rear door, she reached for the phone to call the police. Just as she picked up the receiver, a sound came from out back and she was sure it was the rear door opening. Dropping the phone, she ran across the store, pulled open the front door and hurried across the street, intent on putting as much distance as possible between herself and whoever was breaking into her building.

The screeching sound of brakes had her suddenly looking to her left and freezing in fear, even as her mind was screaming for her to move and get out of the way of the car that was heading towards her. As she threw her hands up to shield her eyes from the blinding headlights, an icy wave of fear washed over her and settled in her stomach. She knew she was going to die and tensed waiting for the impact. Instead, the vehicle slid to a halt, stopping just inches from her. She stared wide-eyed at the bumper that was almost touching her legs. Only once she realized she was safe did she swing her gaze to the driver who was getting out of the car and angrily storming over to her.

"What the hell do you think you're doing, lady? You don't run across the street without looking! I could've killed you!" A large burly man clad in a sweaty T-shirt and stained jeans loomed over her. He spit a wad of tobacco juice on the road beside her.

With a whoosh, she exhaled the breath that she hadn't even known she was holding. "I... I'm sorry. I was working late in the flower shop, and I heard someone trying to break-in through the back door..." She gestured toward her store.

"Did you call the police?"

"N-n-not yet." Stephanie tried to control the chattering of her teeth.

"Geez! Women! You should be home taking care of your men instead running all over creation." Obviously disgusted, he flipped open his cell phone and dialled 911 while grabbing her arm and marching her to the sidewalk. She was sure she'd have bruises on her arm in the morning. "Stay here. I'll move my car and wait with you, but geez lady, now I'm going to be late for the game." He stalked off, phone pressed to his hear, leaving Stephanie standing alone by the street lamp.

Reaction was starting to set in. Her knees lost their strength and began to buckle while everything around her began to grow dark. Gripping the lamp post, she willed herself to stay upright, shivering as the reality of her near miss began to sink in.

Closing her eyes, she prayed the police would arrive soon and hoped the thief hadn't made it to the cash register. She hadn't done the night deposit yet and the thought of losing that much cash filled her with dread. The store was turning a profit and she was getting by, but losing a whole day's take would really mess up her budget. She'd never be able to afford a new fan let alone a new air conditioner. Perhaps she'd made enough noise running out of the store that she'd scared him off before he could steal anything.

"Stephanie?" Seemingly out of nowhere, Jake was beside her, his voice full of concern. "Why are you out here instead of in the store? What's going on?"

"Oh Jake!" Without thinking, she launched herself against him, wrapping her arms around his waist and pressing her face to his chest. Tears began to well up, spilling down her cheeks and she dug her fingers into his back, trying to draw strength from him.

He put his arms around her, holding her close while gently rubbing her back and making soft soothing noises. In some corner of her mind, she noted how good it felt to have someone to turn to, to feel the warmth of another person seeping into her.

"Steph, don't cry. Please. Tell me what's wrong."

Before she could answer, the man from the car reappeared. "This your woman? She's trying to get herself killed or something 'cause she ran right out in front of my car. Good thing I just got the brakes fixed or she'd be dead."

"Dead?" Shock was evident in Jake's voice. He held Stephanie away from him, his fingers biting into her arms as he gazed at her with a mixture of anger and concern. "Steph, did you run in front of his car? What were you thinking? He's right. You could've been killed and I wasn't even here." He gave her a slight shake before pulling her into a tight hug, again.

"If I'd killed her, your being here wouldn't have mattered. Dead is dead, isn't it?" The man spat tobacco juice onto the ground again. "Listen, the police will be here in a minute. I gotta get going—game's starting in ten minutes. You staying with her?"

"Of course." Jake scowled at the man.

"Good. Then I'm outta here." With a final spit, the man left.

Jake eased Stephanie away from him again. "Okay. Now what happened that made you run across the street like that?"

Feeling a bit foolish, Stephanie stepped out of his arms, wiped her face and then shoved her damp hands in her pockets. She stared up at the sky, silently berating herself even as she explained what had happened.

"While I was cleaning up in the back room, I thought I heard someone at the rear door. At first I thought it might have been you, but then I realized that it sounded like someone was working the lock. I started to think about all of the break-ins lately and I panicked, ran out of the store and across the road without looking." She cast a sideways look at Jake. "Dumb, I know."

"Yeah, dumb. But understandable. Are you sure someone was trying to break-in?"

"At the time I was... Now I wonder if I overreacted."

At that moment the police drove up. Two officers exited the vehicle, introducing themselves as Officers Carter and Baker. Stephanie explained the situation and they went to investigate the store while she waited with Jake. Soon one officer exited the shop and crossed the road to where they were standing.

"You were right, ma'am. Someone broke in. The back door is open and there's evidence that the lock was tampered with."

"Is the till open? Did he take the money?"

"I'm afraid so. He seemed to know right where to go. Nothing else appears to have been touched. We'll have you look around to verify that, but it appears that it was a quick in and out job."

"Oh no..." The loss of the money had her stomach clenching. "Do you think it's the same person that's been breaking into the other homes and businesses in town?"

"We can't tell yet ma'am, but it's quite likely. It's the same MO: breaking in at night through a window or door. Going straight for the goods—no random searching. He was probably in your store earlier, posing as a customer and checking the place out." The officer delivered the information in a monotone voice. Obviously this was all routine to him. "We'll need a statement from you, and once they've checked for fingerprints or any other evidence, we'll let you lock up."

"Any idea how long that will be, officer?" Jake spoke for the first time.

"It shouldn't be too long. Probably under an hour. And who are you, sir?"

"Jake St. Clair."

"And your relationship to this lady is...?"

"Acquaintance," Stephanie said.

"Boyfriend," Jake answered simultaneously.

The officer looked from one to the other with a question in his eyes.

"We've just met," Stephanie explained.

"I'm optimistic," Jake added.

"I see." The officer nodded. "Well, you two...friends can wait here or in your car, if it's parked near."

"Mine's right over there." Stephanie pointed to the location of her vehicle.

"All right. If you'd like to wait there, someone will be over to take a statement as soon as possible."

The police officer headed back to the shop and Jake walked Stephanie to her car. She found her keys, opened the door and they climbed in. After sitting in silence for a few minutes, she laughed dryly. "I bet this is the strangest first date you've ever had, isn't it?"

"It does rank up there."

She turned in her seat to face him. "Jake, I'm sorry. You don't have to wait with me. It's late. You've missed your dinner. Go home."

"No. You haven't eaten either. You know this is twice now that I've found you running around hungry. If you're not careful you'll just be skin and bones."

Without meaning to, Stephanie visibly winced at the comment. She was of average size, but comments about her weight still made her uncomfortable. They reminded her of Jarrod Simpson and how he'd taunted her all those years ago. Funny, she hadn't thought of him in ages and now he'd crossed her mind twice in one week.

"Steph?" Jake frowned. "Did I say something wrong? You look unhappy."

"No... It's just that phrase, skin and bones, someone used to tease me about my weight that way."

"Most women would love to have your figure."

"Perhaps, but I was a really skinny 'plain Jane' as a teen and my self-confidence was low." She gave a self-deprecating laugh. "It's silly to let something like that still bother me. Old memories are best forgotten."

"No, not always. Memories of the past help shape the decisions we make today."

"Memories can also hold you back. There are some things I wish I could forget. If I couldn't remember them, I'd be different now."

"How so?" He cocked his head to the side.

"I guess I'd be bolder, more open. Less nervous around new situations or new people." She glanced shyly at him.

"Do I make you nervous?"

"A bit. Actually, I think I'm nervous of myself because this isn't how I usually act. Here I am sitting in a car with a man I barely know and I'm not a bundle of nerves. Well," she paused and tucked a piece of hair behind her ears before qualifying her answer, "except because of the break-in and nearly getting hit by a car. But I'm not nervous of you. I'm not at all sure what's going on in my head right now."

"So usually, if I were to tell you that you're not plain, that you're beautiful and I want to kiss you, you'd be a nervous wreck."

"Something like that." She licked her lips, not totally sure where this conversation was going, but she had her suspicions. The idea intrigued her, which again was so out of character. Darting another glance at Jake, she found he was staring intently at her. Suddenly the interior of the car seemed much smaller and a lot warmer than it had just a minute before.

"Then let's test the theory and see what happens." He reached over and caressed her cheek. "Steph, you are beautiful." His hand slid back under her hair to cup her neck. Gently, he urged her towards him, his eyes locked on hers. When they were but a breath apart he stopped. "Is it all right if I kiss you?"

Lost in his deep blue eyes, she had to replay the question in her mind before comprehending. She nodded her assent and he leaned forward, closing the gap between them.

Jake's lips softly brushed over hers, as if testing her reaction. At first she sat frozen trying to sort out what she was experiencing. His lips were warm and smooth, moving ever so gently against hers. It was pleasant rather than frightening.

Tentatively she moved her lips in response, savouring the sensations that were starting to wash over her. She felt herself melting into a pool of liquid honey. The warmth of his mouth spread through her, and little sparks began to tingle wherever they touched. She pulled away fractionally, wondering if she was just imagining things and then leaned in for a second try.

This time it was like an electric jolt and she gasped at the feeling that coursed through her. As her lips parted, Jake pressed in closer, deepening the kiss. His tongue gently stroked hers then moved away only to return as he changed the angle of the kiss.

Stephanie felt herself sinking into him, becoming lost in the taste and scent and feel of the man. His warm, muscular body pressed against hers; his hair was thick and silky under her fingers. It seemed so familiar, so right, like she'd kissed him a thousand times before…

A tapping on the window, had them quickly pulling away from each other. Officer Carter was standing outside. Stephanie rolled down her window, trying to calm her pounding heart. "Yes Officer?"

"We're ready to take your statement ma'am, and to have you look around the store to see what's missing besides the money from the till."

"I-I'll be right there." She glanced over at Jake and saw that he was looking at her with impatient, hungry eyes. "I have to go..."

"I'm coming with you." It wasn't a question. Just a flat out statement, but Stephanie didn't complain. Having him by her side seemed like the natural thing to do.

Chapter 7

Jake paced the length of Stephanie's living room wondering how he was going to find the strength to leave. The fact that he was in the house already as an invited guest put him way ahead of schedule, but also threw his carefully controlled feelings into disarray. He'd prepared himself not to expect too much too soon, to be satisfied with a hug and chaste kiss; but now that he'd had a glimpse again of the heaven that could be found in Stephanie's arms, how was he going to hold back?

Her reaction to the break-in had been more emotional than he would have expected. When she'd practically thrown herself into his arms when he came up to her on the street corner, he'd nearly groaned out loud. The feel of her warm, slight frame pressing against his, her arms around his waist, her fingers digging into his flesh...

Memories of the last time he'd held her like that had come rushing back to him. It had been all he could do to keep from sweeping her off her feet. Then, in the car, she'd looked so vulnerable. When she had let him kiss her, he'd been elated. She was opening up to him, trusting him. The look in her eyes as she'd stared into his almost made him wonder if she remembered... But, no. It wasn't possible.

After they'd looked over the flower shop and determined that nothing was missing, they'd gone to one of the fast-food chains. They'd sat in yellow plastic chairs at a bright red table. Fluorescent lighting had glared down on them as they ate their hamburgers and fries. Stephanie had just picked at her food and stared distractedly at the imitation flowers that filled the planter beside them. Finally he'd asked if she wanted to go home. Apologetically she'd indicated that she wasn't really hungry and was ready to leave.

She'd refused to let him drive her home and he'd insisted on following her, just to make sure she arrived safely. Outside her house, he'd exited his car, opened her car door and walked her to the front step. Her gaze had traced over his features, a slight frown marring her brow.

"What's the matter, Steph?"

"Nothing... There's just something about you." She'd paused before explaining further. "I'm usually pretty wary around people I don't know, especially men, but it's so different with you. Almost like I already know you, which is silly isn't it?"

"Maybe it's destiny, like I told you the other day."

She'd laughed off his comment, and then hesitantly asked if he'd like to come in for some coffee. Of course, he'd agreed. Her house was small, but sufficient for her needs, she'd explained while showing him the living room and kitchen. He'd made sure his face was politely interested, giving no indication that he'd been there before. The cat had greeted him like the old friend he was, which puzzled her.

"Coco was a stray. She doesn't usually like strangers."

"Animals have always taken to me. I seem to have a natural affinity with them." He'd offered the explanation while kneeling down and rubbing the cat's chin. Coco had been easy to win over during his visits to Stephanie's house. A bit of catnip and the animal had immediately become his friend.

Stephanie had chuckled, obviously pleased that her pet liked him, then made her way to the kitchen where she'd prepared the cat's dinner. He'd watched as she'd taken a pill out of a box on the counter, filled a glass with water, and popped a small tablet into her mouth.

"What was that for?" Instantly he'd been alert to her state of health.

"Allergies. They just started up. The doctor said I could be allergic to Coco, but I hope not; she's all the family that I have. I'm taking these pills to see if it makes a difference, but I'm not a good pill taker. I always forget and when I do take them, I get these weird side effects." She'd been busy making the coffee while she spoke, and had started when she felt his hands on her shoulders, turning her to face him.

"Jake?" Her blue-green eyes had stared up at him, questioning but unafraid.

"Just a minute." He'd held her face in his hands and rubbed his thumbs over her cheeks then across her forehead while looking into her eyes. She'd frowned at him, but didn't try to pull away.

"What are you doing?"

"Checking if you have allergies or not. I think it's probably just a summer cold and will be gone before you know it—maybe even by morning."

"You can't diagnose me by just running your hands over my face."

"Possibly you're right, but I'm very intuitive about things like this and I was checking out your eyes as well. Eyes aren't only the windows to your soul, but also to your health."

"Right..." She'd looked at him quizzically. "So are you into all that 'New Age' and natural healing kind of stuff?"

"Something like that." He'd chastised himself for acting without thinking, and thankfully grabbed onto the explanation she'd offered.

She'd leaned over to open the window and then turned on the ceiling fan. "Are you any good with air conditioners? I'm sorry it's so stuffy in here, but the darn thing broke and I was told it wasn't worth fixing."

"Sorry. I've no talent when it comes to mechanical things. Only living creatures."

"Oh well, just thought I'd ask. Listen, the coffee will be ready in a moment. While it's dripping through, I'll just change into something a bit more comfortable if you don't mind."

He'd raised his eyebrows at her comment and smiled when she flushed after realizing how it had sounded.

"I didn't mean that! Well I did, but not in that way... It's just that I'm really hot..." She'd stumbled over her explanation and he'd debated about teasing her further, but then decided the night had already been eventful enough.

"I know you didn't. I'll just wait in the living room." He'd made sure his smile was gentle and understanding, not wanting her to realize how much he wished there really had been another meaning to her words. She'd given him a grateful look and had hurried down the hall.

Now Jake paced the small room, looking out the front window, examining the pictures on the mantel and wondering why he'd agreed to come in. This was a bad idea. Surrounded by her presence, his senses were becoming heightened and his desire was mounting. He worried that he might not be able to control himself and he didn't want to frighten her. It was too soon.

"I'm back."

He turned and saw Stephanie standing nervously in the doorway. She'd put on denim shorts and a coral tank top , the bright colour adding warmth to her fair complexion. Her feet were bare and her toes were digging into the carpeting as if trying to keep herself grounded.

"That was fast. I like that colour on you."

"Thanks. The coffee is probably ready. Do you want to have it in here on the sofa or in the kitchen?"

"The kitchen's fine." He felt it was safer to stay away from the intimacy of sitting side by side on the couch.

She seemed surprised at his decision, but nodded and headed into the next room. He sat at the table while she got out mugs, cream and sugar. Placing a steaming cup in front of him, she sat across the table and took a sip of the hot beverage.

"It was nice of you to see me home."

"I didn't mind. You still seemed a bit shaken and I wanted to make sure you got here safely."

"It was really unnerving to think I almost came face to face with a thief. I still feel silly for running out of the store like that, though." She made a face. "I probably should have grabbed the broom, waited until he was inside and whacked him over the head."

"That only happens in movies and novels. If you'd stayed, he might have been armed and could have hurt you."

"Armed? None of the police reports have mentioned a weapon." Her eyes widened.

"Well, it just makes sense. The man is committing a crime. He probably has something with him to use in case he's caught.

That's why I'm glad you ran." He reached across the table and held her hand. "You're important to me, Stephanie. I'd hate for something to happen to you."

She stared at him doubtfully. "But you hardly know me."

He rubbed his thumb over the back of her hand. "Believe me, Steph. I know all I need to know."

Shifting uncomfortably in her seat, she pulled her hand away. "Jake, we've only just met. All you know is that I own a flower shop, eat bagels and have a cat that I might be allergic to."

"So tell me then, who is Stephanie Fields and what do I need to know about her?" He grinned and leaned back in his seat.

Obviously surprised to have suddenly been made the topic of conversation, she was slow to respond. "Well... Um... I'm twenty-seven and I own Fields of Flowers, but I guess you know that." He nodded encouragingly, and she took another sip of her coffee before continuing. "I don't have any family. My parents were killed when I was ten and I moved around a lot from one foster home to another until I was about fourteen. Then I went to Mrs. McCreedy's—she ran a foster home for teens—and I stayed there until I aged out of the system. There's not much else to tell—nothing really exciting about me is there?" She shrugged and gave a half laugh, glancing at him briefly before studying her coffee cup again.

"Those are the basics, but I think you left out a lot, like... How did you end up owning a flower shop?"

"Oh that one's easy." She visibly relaxed. "After I left Mrs. McCreedy's, I started working at Weston Flowers—that's what the store used to be called—and I found out that I had an eye for floral design. Then, when Mrs. Peters, the original owner, wanted to retire she asked if I'd like to buy the business. I had a bit of an inheritance from my parents and used it for the down payment." She shrugged. "The bank still owns over half of the shop, but I make enough to pay the mortgage each month and keep a roof over my head."

"So you're a self-starter with a good head for business, an eye for design and a vision for the future."

She blinked. "I beg your pardon?"

"That's what I learned about you from that little tidbit. See, I really do know a lot about you, Stephanie." He took a sip of coffee to hide his smile.

"Well then you have an advantage on me because I don't really know much about you."

"I gave you my references."

"And I checked them out."

"Somehow I knew you would." He smiled at her so she'd know it wasn't a criticism.

"But the references don't tell me much beyond your name, age, job and the fact that you're financially successful. Do you have a family?"

"No, they've been gone for quite a while."

"And where are you from?" She prompted him again.

"All over. Most recently Europe. I've travelled a great deal throughout my life."

"So you've never settled in one place."

"I've had several long stays in various places. I lived in Scotland for quite some time and France."

"It must be fascinating, travelling around the world." Stephanie propped up her chin with her hand and her eyes took on a dreamy wistful look.

"It has its moments, but having someone you care about—setting down roots—that's what's really important."

"And is that why you're in Weston? To set down roots, or is it just a stopover?"

"I think that might depend on you."

As his meaning sank in, she blushed. "Jake—"

"I know, I know. I'm going too fast for you, but when I see something I want I go for it." Noticing that she was at a loss for words, he decided it was best to end the evening. "I'd better go. It's getting late."

Stephanie stood and walked him to the door. "Thanks again for waiting when I said I'd be late, and for dinner." She gave a soft laugh. "And staying when the police came. Wow, that's a lot for a first date, isn't it?"

He smiled. "I didn't mind at all."

"Well, I really appreciated your support."

"I was glad to do it." He gazed down into her eyes. Right now they were more green than blue. They always changed colour when her emotions were up, he recalled. Leaning forward he lightly brushed her lips with his. Her response was immediate and yielding. She leaned into him, her arms creeping up around his neck. The sweet taste of her played over his tongue and it was with great reluctance that he reached up and drew her arms from around him, gently breaking off the kiss and stepping out of her arms. Slowly her eyes drifted open and she stared up at him with a bemused look.

"Jake?"

"Shh." He laid a finger over her lips. "That's enough for tonight. Tomorrow, I'll pick you up from work. We'll have a real dinner out and talk a little bit. Okay?"

"Okay."

"Goodnight Steph. Make sure you lock your doors and windows." He went down the steps and paused at the bottom listening until he heard the deadbolt slide into place. With a nod, he headed to his car. Good, she's all locked up safe and sound for the night.

As he drove home, he speculated as to why things were progressing quicker than he had anticipated. The break-in and the near miss with the car were certainly factors. And, it had been so long since they were together. Perhaps, on some subconscious level, she missed him too. She was already falling for him; he'd had enough experience that he knew the signs. He wondered how she'd react, however, once she knew the truth.

Chapter 8

Stephanie locked the door and leaned against it for a moment wondering what was going on with her. All Jake had to do was touch her and she practically melted. That wasn't like her at all. She was shy and cautious around men, awkward even. Just look at her record-long list of first dates that never led to second dates. But with Jake... She had practically thrown herself into his arms on the street corner and she didn't even know him!

Of course, the break-in was upsetting, and almost being hit by a car was traumatic, but the kiss in her car, and here at the door... She usually only allowed a little peck on the cheek. And she'd asked him in for coffee! Stephanie Fields was above all else cautious and wouldn't let a man she'd just met into her house on the first date, even if he did have great references.

Wandering into the kitchen, she picked up the cups and washed them, turned off the coffee maker and headed down the hall to her bedroom, her mind full of Jake St. Clair. She couldn't believe that someone like him would be interested in her. It wasn't that she was unattractive, she was just...ordinary. There was nothing about her to catch someone's eye. The idea that he'd seen her, and gone into the store to ask Paula about her, just seemed too unlikely to be true. Things like that happened in movies and books, not in real life, and certainly not to people like her.

She flopped onto her bed and contemplated the ceiling. Okay, supposing for some bizarre reason, he really was interested in her. Now what? He'd asked her out again, they'd talk—though for the life of her she couldn't imagine about what. He'd travelled around the world for heaven's sake! She'd spent almost all of her life in Weston, except for a few brief stays in foster homes in the nearby city of St. George and a trip to Florida one winter. She didn't do anything exciting like rock climbing or belly dancing. There'd be nothing to keep his interest. She wasn't even sexy.

Sex was still a big question mark for her. Beyond Jake's kisses, all of her previous experiences had left her unmoved. The attack was partly to blame, but she often wondered if her life would've been much different if that incident hadn't happened. Maybe she just didn't have what it takes. Intellectually the idea of sex interested her, but emotionally and physically, nothing seemed to happen—except in her dreams.

Was sex really the big deal that everybody made it out to be or was it just a lot of propaganda?

Paula seemed to enjoy it, if her exploits were to be believed. The young divorcee had a heart of gold, but went through men like the flower shop went through flowers. There seemed to be a new man in her life every month, and even when the relationship faltered she was only down for a day before bouncing right back into the thick of things. Paula was one of those perfect, perky people. With her black hair, ready smile and bubbly personality, she seemed capable of finding men everywhere, whenever she wanted one.

Sometimes Stephanie fantasized about finding a man who would see her as stunningly beautiful and fascinating. He'd touch her and awaken the woman sleeping inside...

She snorted derisively.

That sounded like something from one of her romance novels. Things like that didn't happen and there was no use pining over it. She was who she was, and her life as it was now, was probably how it was going to be for a good long time. Jake would just be an interesting little interlude in her life. There was no point in building it up into something more. She'd enjoy his attention while it lasted and then have something to look back on when she was old and grey.

Satisfied that she'd come to a bit of a decision about Jake's place in her life, she double checked the locks on the doors and windows, then got ready for bed. The air conditioner was, of course, still broken—unfixable if the repairman was to be believed—and the house was hot and stuffy. One unlocked window wasn't too dangerous, was it? Cracking open the bedroom window, she strategically placed a fan on the table so it would bring in some of the cooler night air.

For a moment she stood looking out. The stars were bright against the black velvet sky and moonbeams seemed to dance through the trees, creating interesting patterns on the lawn. It looked so peaceful.

Coco wandered in and twined herself around Stephanie's ankles. She scooped the cat up into her arms. "Hello sweetie. You were really feeling friendly tonight, weren't you? Did you like Jake?"

The cat patted her face.

"I'll take that as a yes. You know what? I like him too."

Coco shifted in her arms and looked out the window. Her body stiffened and she struggled to get out of Stephanie's arms. Setting the cat down, Steph wondered what had caught the feline's fancy. Her tail was swishing back and forth and she was pacing in front of the screened opening.

"Is there another cat outside? One of your friends—or enemies—from your alley cat days?"

She peered out the window trying to locate the other animal. As she looked, a feeling of unease came over her again. It was the 'someone's watching me' feeling.

There was no one in sight, but she shivered despite the heat. Rubbing her hands over her arms to smooth out the goose bumps that had suddenly appeared, she decided that maybe it would be better to sleep with the window closed tonight; she'd just suffer through the heat. After all, there had been that break-in just down the street...

Giving a final, nervous glance outside, she slid the glass panes shut and pulled the blinds down, so that the view was obscured. Coco jumped down from the ledge and onto the bed, kneading the surface until she felt it was properly prepared and then laying down for a bath.

"That was weird, wasn't it Coco. Did you feel it, too? Sort of cold, like something evil was out there?"

The cat washed unconcernedly, paying no mind to her mistress's comments.

"Perhaps it really is just a side effect of those allergy pills." Steph said it more to convince herself than to inform the cat. "I'll ask the pharmacist about it tomorrow, if I have some spare time. There's always a long list of possible reactions people can have to medication. Maybe paranoia is one of them."

Adding a stop at the drugstore to her mental list of things to do, she climbed into bed and turned off the lights. The fan hummed quietly in the background and sent a gentle breeze whispering over her skin. Stephanie's eyes drifted shut and she imagined what it would be like to have Jake's hands skimming over her heated flesh.

~~~

He stood in the shadow of the trees outside her house, watching as the lights were turned off. The night was warm, too warm for his liking. A breeze drifted over his sweat soaked shirt, helping to cool his body down, but it did little to soothe the fire that burned steadily hotter inside him. She was in there, probably lying on the bed dreaming about her handsome suitor. Women were such idiots, always looking for love and undying devotion from a man, never realizing he was just looking for an easy screw.

Slowly he approached the house, surveying the windows and back door. Everything was locked; he'd seen her checking. Not that it mattered. If he wanted to, he could be in the house in under a minute. And he did want to be in that house, but not just yet. There were still a few more things to wrap up first, a job here and there. But then, once they were taken care of, there'd be time to deal with her.

Standing outside her bedroom window, he could see his reflection in the glass. His blue eyes stared back at him, and his dark hair ruffled faintly in the breeze. Turning his head slightly to the side, he checked out his profile. Straight nose, strong chin—the doctor had done a good job. He'd wondered if Stephanie would've recognized him that first time he'd been in the store, but she hadn't. It was funny how a near fatal traffic accident could turn into a lucky break. With a new appearance and some fake ID, he'd been able to start his life all over.
~~~

Forever In Time

Luck had been on his side again, when he'd found Stephanie after all this time. Who would have believed that she'd still be here in this stupid town this many years later? He'd left long ago, determined to never set foot in Weston again, but after travelling all over, some whim had had him returning. Now that he was here, he was making his stay purposeful. He'd make some money, look up old friends and settle a few scores. Yep, it was finally time. Time for Stephanie Fields to get what she deserved, the stupid bitch.

Chapter 9

First thing in the morning, Stephanie called Paula to tell her about the burglary. In response, Paula gave an outraged squeal that had Stephanie holding the receiver away from her ear. Even at a distance, she could hear her friend's anxious inquiries.

"What? A burglary? Oh Steph, I'm so sorry! Are you okay? Did he damage the store? This is all my fault. If I'd been there, you wouldn't have had to stay late by yourself—"

"Paula, calm down. I'm okay." Stephanie braved bringing the receiver back to her ear. "The break-in would still have happened even if you'd been there and anyway, you needed to take care of Chelsea. Remember, family comes first. Now, how's my god-daughter doing today, anyway?"

Paula could be heard taking a deep, calming breath before responding. "Better. She threw up half the night, but seems fine now. Kids are so resilient. My mom's agreed to watch her so I can go in to work today."

"Only if you're sure. I can manage on my own, otherwise."

"Nope, I'll be there. Besides, I want to find out all the details of your date with Mr. Hot Stuff." Paula then hung up before her boss could reply. Stephanie loved her friend dearly, but she did seem to have a one-track mind when it came to men.

Despite the previous night's burglary, Stephanie felt like she was floating around the shop the whole day. Her sleep had been punctuated with the same steamy dreams that had plagued her of late, but now the man had a face and it was Jake. She was eager to see him again after work, but hoped she wouldn't blush—some of the images in her dream had been quite vivid. In preparation for her date, she'd dressed in her favourite coral blouse and off-white pants, recalling that he'd liked the colour of her tank top the night before. She put on her apron, hoping she could avoid staining the outfit while she worked.

For once, everything seemed to be going perfectly. The flowers for the Johnston wedding were on their way. Paula was back to help, and the traffic flow through the shop was steady, but not overwhelming. The only downturn to the day was that she couldn't find her name tag. She was sure that it had been on the apron when she'd taken it off the night before. After finishing the wedding bouquets, she remembered she'd removed the apron and draped it over her desk chair in the back room. However, the tag was no longer pinned to the material, nor had it fallen onto the top of the desk.

"Maybe it got knocked on the floor when the police were here last night." Paula suggested. The two women crawled on the floor, looking under counters and behind the filing cabinet, but beyond dust bunnies and an old pen, they had no luck.

"Oh well, it was just a name tag." Stephanie said as she slowly surveyed the room.

"Yes, but it was *your* name tag and I remember how proud you were when you could finally put the word 'owner' on it."

"It was the first time that I finally felt like I had something of my own and that I was going somewhere with my life." Steph recalled that day fondly, a smile playing over her lips.

"If it doesn't turn up, I'll get you a new one." Paula whipped the dust from her knees after taking a final look under the counter.

"You don't have to do that, but thanks for the offer." She gave her friend a hug. Just then the phone rang and the front bell jingled. "Back to work. I'll get the phone."

"And I'll get the customer. Maybe it'll be someone like your Jake—tall dark and scrumptious." Laughing, Paula swished through the curtained doorway into the front showroom.

Eight hours later the day finally came to an end. Stephanie had just finished handing her assistant the night deposit when Jake tapped on the door. Paula let him in on her way out.

"See you on Monday, Steph. You two have a fun weekend. Remember to NOT behave." She'd smiled gleefully at Steph's appalled face. Jake just grinned and wiggled his eyebrows.

"I like your friend," Jake said leaning on the counter, watching her finish her work.

"Sometimes I wonder if she *is* a friend or not." Stephanie was still feeling a bit embarrassed about Paula's suggestive comment.

"She just wants you to be happy and enjoy life a little."

"I know. I just wish she'd be a bit more subtle about it." She grabbed an envelope to put Monday's orders in. "Ouch!" Shaking her finger, she popped it into her mouth.

"What?" Jake stood up, a look of concern on his face.

"Paper cut," she mumbled from around her finger.

"Let me see." He withdrew the digit from her mouth and looked at it, carefully running his thumb over the surface, then slowly bringing it to his mouth and kissing it. "There, it's all better now."

"Thanks, but that only works when you're three years old." Stephanie retrieved her finger and studied it critically. "Huh... That's strange. I could have sworn I cut it." She peered at her finger more closely, squeezing the end and examining it for blood or evidence of a break in the skin. Looking up at Jake she frowned. "You saw it, didn't you?"

He shrugged. "Not really. But then again, I was more interested in the opportunity to kiss you, though your finger isn't as satisfying as your lips." With that he leaned forward and brushed his mouth over hers.

Stephanie was sure there must be electric sparks in the air every time he did that. She leaned over the counter, trying to get closer, to deepen the kiss. The counter top dug into her stomach and she had to pull away. "Ugh!" Rubbing her ribs, she looked at him ruefully. "That counter is not conducive to kissing."

"Not when we're on opposite sides," he agreed. "But I think it might be the perfect height if you were on it."

It took a moment for Stephanie to pick up on his meaning and she felt her face redden.

Jake grinned. "Sorry. I couldn't resist."

Despite her embarrassment, Stephanie felt a peculiar thrill at his sexual innuendo. She eyed the counter seeing it in a whole new light.

"I'll pull the blinds for you while you finish up here. Anything else need doing?"

"No. Paula and I had things pretty well wrapped up. I'll just grab my purse and turn out the lights." She gave her head a shake to clear the image of herself on the countertop from her mind.

Jake took her to a quiet restaurant on the edge of town that served a variety of entrées. It was a small establishment, with stucco walls and intimate tables separated by strategically placed plants and bits of lattice.

"I hope this is all right." He was looking a bit anxious as they sat down.

"It's perfect. I've been here a few times and the food is good." She fixed her napkin in her lap. "Actually, I was a bit afraid you'd take me to one of those really fancy places uptown and I'd be too nervous to enjoy myself."

"I'm saving that for date number four."

"Number four? You're so sure there will be a next one?"

"Optimism and a firm belief in destiny are the guiding forces in my life." He winked at her while taking a sip of water. Using his fingers he began to enumerate. "Date number one, a simple exchange of names over coffee. Date number two – a burger and fries. That lets you know that I'm just an ordinary guy, nothing alarming about me. Number three though, requires a bit of a change in strategy. I take you someplace like this. I carefully observe your choices tonight and then, on date number four, we go to some posh restaurant that specializes in what you like, thus overwhelming you with my astute understanding and intuition."

"But you've just told me your plan, so now I won't be impressed on date number four. I'll know what you're up to." She pointed out what she felt was a major flaw in his master plan.

His eyes danced with amusement. "Ah... But now you've agreed that there will be a date number four."

She tried to look affronted. "Oh, now that wasn't nice, tricking me like that."

"All's fair..." He answered smugly.

The waiter appeared and they placed their orders. Jake asked about her day and she told him. "The only real problem all day was that my name tag went missing."

"That little brass one you had on when we went for coffee?"

She nodded. "Uh-huh. It isn't worth much—just sentimental value really. I bought it for myself the day I finalized my mortgage and the shop was officially mine."

"Could it have fallen on the floor?"

"Paula and I searched all over. I don't know where it could have gone. It's not like the thief would have taken it or anything."

"I'm sure it will turn up."

"You're probably right." She took a sip of wine and turned the focus of the conversation onto him. "What did you do today?"

"I checked out a few prospective office spaces and started to make some contacts."

"So you're really going to set up shop in Weston?"

"I told you I would."

"I guess I just can't see why anyone would choose to come here. I mean, it's a nice town and all but..." She let her voice trail off and shrugged.

"I already told you why I'm here—you." He reached across the table and took her hand in his. Stephanie stared into his eyes, not sure what she was searching for. Sincerity? Love? There was something about the way he looked at her, like he knew her, *really* knew her.

Their food arrived and the moment was lost. At first, talk was general—about books, TV and the weather. She asked his opinion about getting a new air conditioner. He inquired how her cold was today and she reminded him it was allergies. They laughed and argued over the diagnosis, but finally agreed that it didn't matter since she hadn't had any sniffles all day, even without taking the allergy pills.

She questioned him about his travels and he spoke of countries he'd visited. It turned out Jake was interested in history and could give amazingly detailed information about the places he'd been, painting pictures with his descriptive words and anecdotes. Yet he never made her feel less important for her own limited experiences, instead drawing her in and asking her opinions. When the meal was over, Jake drove her back to the flower shop to get her car then followed her home again and walked her to her door.

"Do you want to come in for coffee again?" She asked him hopefully, not wanting the night to be over.

He brushed the back of his fingers against her cheek. "Do I want to come in? Yes. Will I come in? No."

"I don't understand."

"I'd like nothing more than to go inside, but if I do, I won't want to leave and you aren't ready for that yet, are you?"

"Oh." She felt confused as the idea of him staying had great appeal. His arms around her, his body pressed tightly to hers while his lips roamed over her. But at the same time, her mind sent up warning signals. If they started, would she be able to go through with it or would old fears and memories raise their ugly heads?

"See what I mean? You're not sure. Soon, but not quite yet." He brushed his lips lightly across hers then stepped back. "Lock the doors, Steph, and I'll call you tomorrow."

She locked the door and wandered into the kitchen, her mind focused on Jake. He was so nice and he made her feel, well... She wasn't sure what, but it was something. This must be that tingly, giddy feeling the heroines always talk about in my books, she told herself. Looking around, she wondered where Coco was. It was way past her supper time and the cat should be whirling around her ankles, complaining about being neglected.

"Coco? Dinner time." Hitting the edge of the can with a spoon, she figured that would have the beast running into the kitchen. When the cat didn't appear, she set the food down on the floor and went looking for her, checking all of her the favourite hiding spots. She looked under the sofa and chair, then behind the washer and dryer—no cat. Heading down the hallway, she checked the spare room and then looked under her own bed. Still no cat.

Turning, she slowly surveyed the room, finally noticing that the closet door was slightly ajar.

"Coco? Come on out, sweetie. It's just me." A faint rustling sound heralded the arrival of the cat into the room. The feline slunk out, her belly dragging on the ground. "Oh dear, what's the matter, Coco?" Stephanie crooned and bent to pick up the cat, rubbing her chin and behind her ears, talking to her in a soothing voice. Of course the animal didn't answer, but it did bury its face in her neck. Frowning, Stephanie carried her cat into the kitchen and set her down in front of her food, wondering what had spooked her.

Once on the floor, Coco ignored her meal and immediately headed back towards the bedroom. Following the cat, Stephanie watched as it jumped onto the bed, pacing back and forth, sniffing the spread, her tail slightly fluffed.

Steph looked at the bed, wondering what the cat was doing. Coco began clawing at the bedspread that covered her pillow. There seemed to be a lump there, and she wondered if there could be a mouse hiding under the cover. She shivered at the thought, but forced herself to walk towards the bed. Slowly and carefully she grabbed the edge of the sheet and mentally counted to three before yanking the cover back, prepared to jump away if a rodent was indeed hiding there. Instead, she saw her pillow, with her name tag on it, the pin part impaling a photograph of herself.

Chapter 10

By the time Jake arrived back at Stephanie's house, the police were already there. At first, they weren't even going to let him in, but then Officer Carter recognized him from the previous night and ushered him inside. Stephanie was sitting on the sofa cradling a cup of coffee, while a female police officer sat beside her asking questions.

"Steph?"

She glanced up and immediately held out her hand, half rising, her eyes appealing for his help. "Jake, I'm so glad you're here." Her voice trembled and her face was pale.

"I came as soon as I heard your message on my voice mail. What's going on?"

The police woman interrupted. "Sir, if you could just wait a moment, I need to finish taking her statement."

He was about to protest, but Stephanie nodded. "It's okay, Jake. I'd just like this to be over."

Sitting beside her, he gripped her hand tightly and listened as she related the events. "So after I found the cat, I brought her into the kitchen, but she wouldn't eat, she just went back into the bedroom, jumped on the bed and started sniffing around. I saw a lump under the bedspread and thought it might be a mouse so I pulled it back and that's when I saw it."

"And what exactly did you see, ma'am?"

There was a faint quiver in Stephanie's voice as she spoke and she held his hand tightly. "A picture of myself on my pillow and my missing name tag. The pin part was stabbed into my face."

The officer didn't show any emotion, she just continued jotting down the information. "And where is the name tag usually?"

"I usually wear it at work. I keep it there, too. But I couldn't find it today. There was a break-in at the flower shop last night and this morning I noticed that the tag was gone."

"So to the best of your knowledge the name tag went missing at work and somehow ended up in your bedroom. You didn't accidentally bring it home."

"No. I never do that. Someone must have taken it from the shop, broke into my house and put it on my pillow, along with the picture."

"Do you know how this person got in?" The officer looked up from her notes.

Stephanie shook her head. "The front door was locked when I came home. I didn't check the back door or windows."

The policewoman looked at another officer who was standing in the doorway. He nodded and left only to return a minute later with a report. "Same MO. The lock on the back door was picked."

"Is anything missing? Jewellery? Money? Electronics?" The police woman prodded, her pencil poised ready to make a list.

"No. Nothing in my bedroom looked different. The dresser drawers were all closed just as I'd left them, and I only have costume jewellery. No one would mistake it for the real thing. There was no money in the house." Stephanie glanced around the living room. "My TV is still here, and the computer is over there in the corner. There's nothing else worth taking."

"All right. So nothing is missing. Do you remember when this picture was taken?" The picture was now housed in a plastic evidence bag and the officer held it up for her to see.

"No, not really. I didn't look that closely at it, but I hate having my picture taken so I should remember but..." She shook her head.

"Okay, so we can assume it was probably a candid shot, taken without your consent or awareness. Do you recognize anything in the background of the photo? Something that would give us a hint as to where it was taken?"

"No. Well…" She squinted and peered at the picture. "There's something sort of yellow behind me in the picture, like the sunflower poster on the wall in my flower shop. Is that any help?"

"Possibly. At least it's a start. We'll have the boys in the lab enlarge the photo and go over it." The woman made a few more notes, and then closed her book. "That will be all for tonight. If we need anything else, where can we contact you?"

"She'll be at my place." Jake interrupted. Both Stephanie and the officer looked at him. "You're not staying here by yourself."

"But Coco…"

"She can come too."

Steph stared at him for a moment before squeezing his hand and nodding. "Thanks. I really don't want to spend the night alone in this house, knowing some strange person has been wandering around in it while I'm at work."

Jake gave the officer his number and then put his arm around her shoulders, hugging her gently as they waited for the police to finish their jobs.

At his apartment, Stephanie wandered around, touching the sofa, looking at the paintings on the walls. He watched her for a moment before defending the decor. "I rented it fully furnished. Not much of this stuff is mine."

"I wondered. Beige sofas and cheap reprints don't strike me as your style." She wrapped her arms around herself then stood looking out the balcony doors.

He walked up behind her and gently laid his hands on her shoulders. Giving them a squeeze, he eased her back so that she was leaning against him. "Do you want to talk about it?"

"Not really. I mean, I guess I do, but I don't. Does that make any sense?" She glanced over her shoulder at him.

"Not really." He gave her a half smile and led her to the sofa. "Care to explain?"

She clasped her hands tightly together and stared at her laced fingers. "I really don't want to talk about it—I want to forget that it even happened—but I can't because it *did* happen. Who wants to think about some sicko out there stabbing your picture? Why would someone do that? Why pick me?" She looked up at Jake, her eyes wide, her voice faintly trembling with fear.

"Because he saw your name tag when he broke in and thought it would be fun to scare you. People like that don't operate on a level that we understand." Jake clasped his warm hands over her cold ones and rubbed them.

"But how did he get a picture of me? And when?"

"Who knows?" He shrugged. "You're busy in the shop all day. I'm sure it would be easy for someone to snap a photo with their phone without you noticing. It could even have been while you were shopping in the mall or at the library. You were just guessing when you said it was in the flower shop. With a zoom lens the person could actually have been quite far away." Jake pulled her back so that she was tucked up beside him. He put his arm around her shoulders while his other hand held hers, stilling the nervous movements of her fingers. She sighed and leaned her head back against the cushions.

"I know and that's even scarier. It's like he's stalking me. But why?"

"Steph, I know this is a silly question but, did you ever do anything that got someone in trouble so they'd want to seek revenge? Maybe a car accident or pointing out someone in a line-up? Have you ever accused someone of a crime?"

"No, I've never done anything like that—my life isn't that exciting." She stared at the ceiling and shook her head. "This is just great. I come home from a wonderful evening out and the whole thing is ruined by some weirdo."

"Was it a wonderful evening?"

She rolled her head towards him and reached up to caress his face. "It was. You make me feel happy. Excited. I can't explain it, but it's like I've been waiting for you all my life."

"It's that fate I've been telling you about." He stroked her hair, and then closed his eyes as her fingers trailed over his mouth. The feel of her voluntarily touching him was almost too much. His body quivered and he drew in a ragged breath then abruptly stood up.

"Look, I'll sleep out here. You can have the bedroom."

"Jake, you don't have to." There was a longing in her eyes. He wanted to respond to it oh so badly, but not tonight. The police might call and he didn't want to be interrupted.

"It's not a good idea, Steph. If we start something tonight, I won't be able to stop and you've had an upsetting evening." He softened his rejection with a tender smile. "Come on, I'll show you where the bathroom is and get you a towel. Did you pack a toothbrush? I'm afraid I don't have any spares, since I just moved in, but we could share."

"Thanks, but I think I have everything I need. What about Coco?"

"Her litter box is on the balcony and I'll leave the door cracked open. It won't hurt for once even if the air conditioner is on."

"I'll have to leave the bedroom door open; she usually sleeps with me, but who knows? She's taken quite a shine to you. You might be lucky enough to have a cat walking over you all night."

"I can hardly wait." His voice was laced with playful sarcasm.

She laughed. "Thanks for putting up with me and my cat. You're a nice man, Jacob St. Clair."

"I'm glad you think so. Everyone might not agree with you."

"I can't imagine anyone disliking you, but," she laid her finger over his mouth, "don't tell me about them if they do indeed exist. I'd like to keep my illusions for a while."

He'd studied her for a moment, thinking if she only knew how close to the truth she was. Then quirking a smile, he finished the grand tour of the apartment and bid her goodnight.

Later that evening, Jake stood in the doorway, watching her sleep. Her strawberry-blond hair was spread over the pillows and her pink lips were slightly parted. With his eyes, he caressed her cheek bones, the column of her neck, and the faint swell of her breasts just visible through the V-necked nightgown. She looked so peaceful, so innocent, sleeping in his bed.

His hand gripped the door frame and he fought an internal battle to stay where he was, when his body was urging him to join her. Closing his eyes, he recalled the feel of her body pressed to his, her hands on him, his mouth crushing hers, his fingers tangling in her hair.

He took a step forward, but then stopped himself. No, she had to come to him. There was no other way. Once he'd done it differently and it hadn't worked. The end had been disastrous. If nothing else could be said about his existence, he learned from his mistakes. Patience did pay off and the payoff would be well worth the wait.

"Good night, Stephanie. Don't keep me waiting too long."

Chapter 11

Stephanie awoke with a start, momentarily confused as to where she was. She was facing an off-white wall instead of the pale peach of her bedroom and the pillow case was green striped rather than floral. The familiar scent of her fabric softener was missing too, replaced by a faint spicy scent.

She sat up and looked around, brushing her tangled hair from her face. Having moved around so much as a child, she hated waking up unsure of where she was. Old insecurities rushed to the surface as her gaze darted around the room, and her brain tried to make sense of the unfamiliar venue. Seeing her overnight bag and Coco's carrying crate in the corner, things suddenly clicked into place and she gave a sigh, sinking back down onto the pillow.

Staring at the ceiling, she recalled the events of the previous night and tried to reason out what had happened. Who would do such a thing? So far, the rash of break and enters had been just that—theft was the main focus, but this, this was different. Nothing had been taken from her home. Why was the thief suddenly changing tactics and targeting her?

Something Jake had said last night came back to her. Had she ever done something that would make a person want to seek revenge on her? Wracking her brain, she came up blank. Sure, she'd messed up a few flower orders, but no one could be that upset over a bouquet. Her life was pretty ordinary. No drama, no spurned lovers, not even a traffic ticket. Was it possible that it was just random? Had someone noticed her on the street and thought she looked vulnerable—an easy target? Was some sick person going to start stalking her for their own personal enjoyment, secretly laughing as she became more and more frightened?

A shiver ran through her and suddenly she recalled that was how she'd felt years ago when Jarrod Simpson had tormented her as a teenager. She'd become increasingly nervous, fearful and withdrawn. He'd lapped it up. The more she'd retreated, the more he'd advanced until finally, when she'd broken down and told someone that he...

The memory made her close her eyes and her body tensed. Breathing deeply, she forced herself to finish the thought.

He'd tried to rape her.

For a moment she relived the feelings of helplessness and terror, then forced herself to think beyond that one awful moment. Yes, he'd tried, but he hadn't succeeded, and that was the important thing to remember. She'd fought back, and in the end, he had been taken away and had never bothered her again.

Unknowingly, she set her chin and narrowed her eyes. That's what she would have to do this time. If history was repeating itself, she wouldn't be a victim again. She would stand up to whoever this person was. She wouldn't back down or show fear. It might get a bit messy, but in the end, she'd be a survivor, just like last time. Ella had stood by her all those years ago, and now she had Jake. Somehow, she was certain he'd support her. Jake would keep her safe and help her be strong.

Just thinking about the new man in her life helped her relax and a smile curved her lips. He'd been so kind and concerned last night; hugging her and holding her hand, not assuming that she'd sleep with him just because she was at his apartment. Not that the idea hadn't crossed her mind. But somehow Jake had known she wasn't ready; that she was too emotionally wrought from the night's events to make such an important decision. He really was special.

She stretched luxuriously, marvelling at the fact that she was lying in his bed. The pillow smelled of his shampoo and cologne. His sheets were covering her body, caressing her legs and arms—the very same sheets that had probably covered him the night before. The idea was stimulating and she moved restlessly. The smooth material brushed over her legs, whisper soft like a lover's caress. Closing her eyes, she moved about a bit and imagined the feel of the sheets against her skin was actually his hands sliding over her.

"Steph? Are you up?" The voice was accompanied by a knock on the partially opened door.

The sound of Jake's voice had her bouncing up, clutching the sheet to her chest and turning bright red with embarrassment. Had he seen her moving about? Did he know what she'd been thinking?

He poked his head through the doorway. "Hi! I heard you moving around and figured you were awake. I just wanted to let you know that there's coffee made. I have to go out and get some bread. I wasn't expecting company and the larder is a bit bare."

"Okay. I'll get up and dressed while you're gone." She plucked nervously at the sheets, not quite meeting his eyes.

"Did you sleep all right? No bad dreams?" He took a step into the room and she could feel his gaze upon her. Bracing herself, she looked up and saw concern in his eyes. Maybe he hadn't noticed.

"I slept well, thanks. And you?"

"Coco paid me a few visits, but otherwise good. Despite its looks, the couch is surprisingly comfortable." He paused and checked his watch. "I'll leave you to get dressed. The store's not far from here so I'll probably be gone less than half an hour. I can't imagine the line being too long this early on a Sunday morning."

He left the room and Stephanie buried her face in her hands. Thank heaven he hadn't noticed her writhing about under the sheets. As the sound of the outer door closing met her ears, she threw back the covers and headed for the bathroom, anxious to be dressed and self-composed when he returned.

Adjusting the water, she stripped off her nightgown and stepped under the spray. Warm water cascaded over her body, and she stood for a moment just enjoying the sensation before reaching for the soap and lathering up. Her hands slid over her arms and breasts, down her stomach and back up. Her skin seemed overly sensitive this morning and the relaxing pulse of the water, combined with the smooth feel of soap sliding over her body, had her eyelids becoming heavy.

She was in Jake's shower, using his soap. He'd stood here, naked, just shortly before her; his hands moving over his body just as hers were doing now. What would it feel like to have his hands on her? To have him standing behind her in the shower, his wet body hugging hers? Would she feel the evidence of his desire pressing against her, his breath hot on her neck while his hands stroked her? Her heartbeat quickened at the idea and she felt an ache low down in her body.

Jake was the one, she was sure of it. It was barely four days since they'd met, but she was inexplicably drawn to him. Her body responded to his like it had never done before. She liked how calm and patient he was, understanding and considerate. He wasn't trying to rush her.

Stepping out the shower, she dried herself off while still enumerating his virtues. He was intelligent, upbeat and had a quirky sense of humour. He was ambitious, well off, good looking... Walking into the bedroom, she saw Coco lounging on the bed. And her cat liked him too! What greater endorsement could there be than that?

Laughing at herself, she got dressed, put her hair up in a clip and then went in search of the coffee he'd told her about. Checking the clock, she realized it had only been twenty minutes since he'd left. She wandered around the apartment, and then stared thoughtfully at the phone. Suddenly she had an overwhelming urge to talk to Ella. Dialling the number from memory, she wandered onto the balcony and watched the cars moving on the street below while waiting for the other woman to answer.

"Hello?" The sound of the woman's voice brought an immediate smile to her face as memories of being loved, of belonging, filled her.

"Hi Ella. It's me, Stephanie."

"Stephanie! It's good to hear your voice. How are you, Honey?"

"I'm good Ella and you?"

"Not too bad. My knee still gives me some trouble, but the doctor says a few more weeks of physiotherapy and I'll be right as rain." Ella had had knee surgery recently and been forced to use crutches to hobble about much to the active woman's chagrin.

"That's great, Ella. Is there anything I can do for you? Run some errands?"

"No, I'm fine. My neighbours are helping me out. What you can do, however, is tell me what's going on with that flower shop of yours. I saw in the paper that there was a break-in."

"Yeah. I lost the day's take, but nothing else. Well, my name tag went missing, but I got it back. Sort of."

"Now Honey, that's too bad. But you got the name tag back? I remember the day you came and showed it to me. You were so proud."

"I was."

"So how did you 'sort of' get it back?"

"Well, that's the not so good part. The police have it right now to check for finger prints." Stephanie went on to explain what had happened.

"You didn't stay at home alone last night, did you?" Concern laced the woman's voice. "You know you can come here any time. I always have room for one more."

"No, I stayed the night with a friend."

There was pause on the other end. "A friend? Like a boyfriend?"

Stephanie felt herself blushing. "Yes, a boyfriend, but he slept on the couch."

"Oh." Another pregnant pause filled the air. "Stephanie, that incident with that awful Jarrod boy—"

"Ella, don't worry about it. I'm fine."

"You never finished that counselling. You know it's never too late—"

"Ella, don't fuss. It's okay. It happened a long time ago, and it's over and forgotten."

"Not so forgotten if your boyfriend sleeps on the couch."

"Ella!"

"Honey, I've raised teenagers for more years than you've been alive. I know what happens between young folk, and in this day and age, that's not how things usually work. I might not approve, but I know how things are."

"Ella, I've only known him for four days!"

"And you already agreed to stay at his apartment? Well, I guess all things considered, for you that's a pretty big step. So, you really like him?"

"Yeah, I do. He makes me feel..." She struggled to find the right words. "I can't explain it. Happy. Excited. Alive. I can't wait to see him again."

"Sounds like you're falling for him."

"I think so, too."

"Good! It's about time. Now, back to the break-in at your house. Do the police have any leads?"

"No. Jake, my...my boyfriend." She paused and derisively rolled her eyes at herself for stumbling over the word. "He wondered if there was someone in my past who had a grudge against me, but I can't think of anyone. I think it's just some weirdo who picked me at random."

"Steph, what about Jarrod Simpson?"

"What about him?"

"He has a grudge against you. He ended up in a juvenile detention centre because he attacked you."

"But that was years ago!"

"I know, I know. But he was a strange one. There was something about his eyes. And sometimes when he talked, it was like he was two different people, like voices were telling him things."

Stephanie frowned and bit her lip. "Do you know where he is now?"

"Last I heard he'd left the area after getting out. Oh, and wait, I think I read somewhere that he'd been in a car accident, a real bad one and they didn't know if he'd make it or not. I'm not sure what the outcome was, though."

"Well, I guess I can mention it to the police and see what they think." She turned around and saw Jake standing behind her. "I've got to go, Ella. Jake is back. I'll talk to you later. Love ya."

"I love you, too, Honey. Take care."

"I will. Bye." She returned the phone to its base and Jake gave her a peck on the cheek.

"Sorry I was gone so long. It took longer than I thought—lots of early morning shoppers."

"That's all right, I hadn't noticed. I hope you didn't mind that I used your phone while you were gone. It was a local call."

"That's fine. Who did you feel a need to talk to? Paula?"

"No. Ella McCreedy. She was my foster mother from the time I was fourteen. We've stayed in touch. She's the closest thing I have to family."

He nodded in understanding. "And what do you need to tell the police?"

Stephanie bit her lip and looked away. She didn't tell people about the attack. Paula and Ella were the only ones who really knew. Yet, if she was hoping to have a serious relationship with Jake, he really should know about her past.

"This isn't easy for me to say." She moved to sit on the sofa and stared at the floor. Intellectually, she knew she had nothing to be ashamed about, that being attacked wasn't her fault, but she still didn't want to see the shocked look on his face when she told him.

Jake sat beside her. "It's okay, Steph. You can tell me anything." He gave her a quick one armed hug. The warmth of his touch gave her the courage to speak.

"There was this boy at Ella's. He was another foster kid. His name was Jarrod Simpson. He, um, well, he was always picking on me, making rude comments. Suggestive comments." She stared at her hands, noting how she was twisting her fingers. She clasped them together to force herself to stop. "I started to get really nervous around him—scared actually—and then one day a school counsellor found out about it. She told Ella, and Ella called Social Services to have him moved to another home. Jarrod found out and was really mad at me for squealing on him. He... Well... He attacked me."

"Attacked you?"

She nodded, still staring at the floor.

His voice was hard and cold. "What exactly do you mean by 'attacked' you?"

Stephanie glanced up at Jake. His face was dark, his brows lowered. It made her nervous for some reason. He looked rather formidable; quite unlike the calm gentle person she'd seen thus far. "He…he hit me."

"Is that all?" His voice sounded cold, flat.

"N-no." This was the worst part, having to actually say what he did. "I tried to get away. I hit him and he shoved me. I fell and then he kicked me, punched me, pinned me down. I tried to fight back. When he kissed me I bit him and screamed. He...he ripped my top and was touching me…"

She could hear her voice trembling and tears were welling in her eyes as she related the event. Telling Jake was harder than she'd thought it would be. It was like it had just happened, every sensation still fresh in her mind; the sound of Jarrod's heavy breathing, the feel of his hands, even the smell of his breath.

Inhaling deeply, she pushed the memories away and forced herself to continue. "Then Ella came and some of the older kids pulled him off me, and then... He was gone." She sniffled and, realizing her nose was drippy, glanced around for a tissue. Seeing a box on the end table, she stood to get one and blew, then wiped her eyes. Turning around, she discovered that Jake had also moved and was looking out the balcony doors, his back to her. His hands were fisted at his sides and his back was stiff. "Jake?"

For a moment he didn't respond, she watched his shoulders move as if he was taking a deep breath, forcing himself to relax. He turned to face her and the angry look was gone, replaced by one of concern. Walking over, he gently embraced her. "Steph, that was a terrible experience for you."

"Yeah—it was. I went to a couple of counselling sessions, but it was too upsetting so I quit. I've read some self-help books and mostly I'm okay now. It's not something I like to think about very often, though. What happened is in the past."

"But it still affects you, doesn't it?"

"No. Yes. Well, not that much. I guess I'm more cautious about relationships than some other people." She shrugged not wanting to get into the fact that she'd never been able to go past 'first base' without freezing up. With Jake that feeling of fear wasn't present and, unless she had to, she didn't want to talk about it yet. It was embarrassing to be a twenty-seven year old virgin. She'd have to tell him, if their relationship progressed, but she'd hold off as long as possible.

Jake leaned back and tipped her chin up, studying her carefully. For a moment, she was afraid he'd press for more details, but then, almost as if he already knew her darkest secrets, he brushed his thumb over her cheek and drew her close, pressing a kiss to the top of her head before resting his chin there and hugging her.

It felt good to have his arms around her, to feel his warmth seeping into her, chasing away old demons. She relaxed against him and shut her eyes, her arms creeping around his waist. His hand rubbed up and down her back, and she slowly exhaled as the tension, brought on by reliving the past, drained away.

After a while, he broke the comfortable silence between them. "So why were you going to tell the police this? Surely it's already on record somewhere."

She could hear his voice rumbling deep in his chest as he spoke and, for some reason, it made her smile despite the seriousness of the conversation. "Well, I was telling Ella what had happened last night and how you had wondered if anyone had a grudge against me. She said Jarrod might because he ended up in custody. I think it's a long shot, but I'll mention it to the police, just in case."

"I agree. You never know when something little might help break a case. Call the police and let them check it out but first, how about we have some breakfast?" He eased her back so they were looking at each other. The care and concern in his face filled her with happiness and she smiled up at him, making no effort to hide the emotion in her eyes.

"Sounds like a good idea. I'm starving."

Chapter 12

After fixing them a breakfast of eggs and toast, Jake had listened while Stephanie called the police. Officer Carter agreed that after almost ten years, the likelihood of Jarrod Simpson returning was slim, but agreed it never hurt to follow up on a lead, no matter how old. He also told her that there had been no prints on her name tag and she was free to collect it at the station whenever she wished. As she hung up the phone, she told Jake that she wondered if she really wanted the name tag back or not. It had always been special to her, but now it seemed tainted.

Jake tried to remain neutral about the incident. His real feelings weren't open to public scrutiny at this point. Instead, he changed the topic and they spent some time trying to decide how to spend the day. He felt it should be something calm and relaxing that would take her mind off things.

"We could walk in the park. I think there's an art display today," he suggested as he placed the last of the breakfast dishes in the dishwasher.

"Or maybe go to the conservation area. They have some nice walking trails." Stephanie spoke over her shoulder as she wiped off the counter.

"I know." He came up behind her and placed his hands on her shoulders. "Why don't we go to the beach? It's going to be a scorcher; perfect weather for some sun and surf."

"Okay, I like that idea. I haven't gone in ages. But we'll have to stop by the house to get my bathing suit."

He turned her in his arms. "Not into skinny dipping?"

"Jake!" Stephanie tried to look shocked, but he could tell she enjoyed his teasing by the smile that kept trying to form on her lips.

"All right." He pretended to be annoyed. "Your house is on the way. I guess we could make an extra stop."

Stephanie volunteered to finish cleaning up while he found his trunks, towels and some sunscreen. In less than an hour they were on their way.

It was only about forty-five minutes to the beach. As they drove, Stephanie sang along with various recording artists on the radio. When she caught herself doing it the first time, she'd stopped and apologized, but he'd told her to continue. He liked the sound of her voice and the way she picked up on the feeling of each song. So much emotion was trapped inside her. He could hardly wait to set it free.

He sensed a subtle change in her over the past few days. After being so uptight that first time they'd talked in the flower shop, he was surprised by how relaxed she was around him now. In fact, she seemed to be seeking opportunities to reach out to him. She'd brushed against his arm as they'd walked down the hall, reached for his hand in the elevator and smiled up at him so trustingly. He'd thought, given her past, it might take a while for her to warm up to him, but now he wasn't so sure. Their relationship was progressing quickly. If things went as he hoped, this afternoon would provide a perfect opportunity to see how comfortable she really was around him.

By the time they arrived at the beach, the sun was at its zenith. Waves of heat shimmered across the sand causing the images of the distant beachgoers to waver and blur like a mirage. In contrast, the bright blue of the water beckoned, waves lapping gently at the shore, caressing and cooling the sand before pulling back only to repeat the gesture once again. A few gulls soared overhead, riding the hot air currents and calling to each other as they searched for food.

Jake took it all in as he and Stephanie walked across the pavement of the parking lot, arms laden with towels. To a casual observer they probably appeared like a normal couple, no different from the dozens of others who had gathered here today. A normal couple. The idea made his lips twitch with amusement.

"How about over there?" Stephanie pointed out a location on the sand and he nodded amiably following in her wake. The breeze was lightly stirring her hair and he took a moment to admire how the strawberry-blond tresses shimmered in the sun. He remembered how it felt in his hand. Soon. Soon he'd be able to run his fingers through it, use it to hold her head in place.

"Jake?" With a start he realized she'd asked him a question and, taking his cue from the towel she was holding, helped her spread it out on the sand.

Surprisingly, the beach wasn't too crowded and the spot Stephanie had chosen offered some semblance of privacy. Good. That was what he needed if his plans for the day were to work.

Stephanie had put her suit on at her house and now she hesitantly peeled off her shirt and shorts. The orange flowered tankini hugged her body, showing off her slim frame and gently swelling curves. His eyes moved from the spaghetti straps, to the conservative neckline down to where just a strip of her tummy showed and a tantalizing glimpse of her navel could be seen. The boy cut shorts suited her long legs and trim hips.

"Very nice," he commented as he casually stripped down to his trunks.

She looked at him and smiled shyly. "You look pretty good, too."

He smirked at her comment and struck a quick pose then grabbed the bottle of sunscreen. "Your skin's so fair. You'd better put on some of this." He squirted some into his own hands before giving her the bottle. As he rubbed the protective lotion onto his arms, he watched her do her own arms and upper chest. She sat down and squirted more lotion onto her legs. His hands slowed and then stopped moving completely as he watched her smooth sunscreen up and down her long, shapely limbs.

"Jake?"

"Hmm?" With a start, he realized that he'd been staring and grinned unrepentantly at her.

"Would you do my back?"

"I thought you'd never ask!" He winked at her and gave a wolfish grin. Sitting behind her, he smoothed the lotion over her shoulders, sliding his fingers under the straps and then working his way down to the edge of the tank top. A small strip of her lower back was also exposed and he applied sunscreen there as well, his hands sliding around her sides, venturing onto her belly before returning to her back. Her stomach muscles had contracted under his touch and he repeated the move, before sliding his hands even lower, tracing the moon shaped birthmark on her upper thigh, while a finger from his other hand dipped into her navel. A shiver swept over her and he whispered in her ear. "I've always loved your birthmark."

"Always? You've never seen it before." She craned her neck to see him, questioning his choice of words.

"Right. I meant I've always liked the crescent symbol for the moon." Seeking to distract her, he handed her the bottle of lotion. "My turn now."

"Pardon?"

"My turn. I put sunscreen on your back, now you put sunscreen on mine. That's how it works."

"Oh, sure." She moved so that she was behind him. The cool lotion on his back made him jump, but then the warmth of her hands moving over his skin soon had him biting back a groan. Her fingers played over his shoulders, back and forth, up and around to skim his collarbone, then back down. He felt himself relaxing under the soothing rhythm and was surprised to realize how tense he was. The past few months had been hard, but he'd done this before, he should be used to it by now. Perhaps he was getting old, he thought sardonically.

As if she'd read his thoughts, Stephanie stopped with her hands still on his back. "Jake, your muscles are awfully tight. Why don't you lie down and I'll give you a massage? I'm really good at them. Paula swears by them."

"Sure. I was just thinking that I didn't realize how tense I was." He stretched out on the towel and she began to work her thumbs into the knots. This time he let the groan escape. "Aaah, Steph. That feels so good. Where'd you learn to do that?"

"Ella, my foster mother, used to get really sore shoulders." She laughed softly at the memory. "It was probably tension from all of those teenagers running around. Anyway, I'd give her shoulder massages. She said I had a natural talent for them."

"Mmm. You can use your natural talents on me any time you like." He closed his eyes and, for the first time in weeks, just concentrated on feeling. No strategizing. No second guessing. No setting up circumstances to work in his favour. It was a relief to just be a regular person for change. 'This is what it will be like, once things are settled with Steph,' he thought to himself.

He wasn't sure how much time had passed before he realized that Stephanie was no longer working the kinks out of his muscles. Her fingers had been replaced by something else. Feather-like kisses were trailing down his spine and her hair was brushing over him like the wings of an angel. "Steph." Her name rumbled out of his throat on a warning note.

"What?" There was a hint of teasing in her voice.

"That's not a back massage."

"Very good, Mr. St. Clair. Ten points for the astute observation." She giggled, her breath tickling his back.

He rolled over and saw that she was stretched out beside him. The sun was behind her and he had to squint to see. "What do you think you're doing?"

"You tell me." Her head blocked the sun as she leaned over him. Gently, her mouth moved over his, the pressure light, exploring. He responded in kind, letting her take the lead, curious to know how far she'd go. Her tongue was tracing the seam of his lips, asking for more. He opened and her tongue slid in, stroking his, causing feelings long suppressed to come rushing to the surface.

Of their own volition, his hands moved to her waist, pulling her over on top of him. The feel of her nearly naked body pressing down onto his was exquisite torture and he allowed his hands to roam hungrily over her back, pushing the tankini up so he could feel her bare skin.

Rolling them over so that she was under him, he tugged the material of her top out of the way and cupped the soft mounds of her breasts. She was so warm and soft and willing under him. Her hands gripped his back, pressing him closer. The blood pounded through his veins and he knew he had to have her.

It was the sound of laughter, and a child's screams of delight, that finally broke through the haze of desire that had swept over him. He pulled away and shook his head to clear it.

"Jake?" She looked up at him with unfocused eyes. Her mouth was parted and she was breathing heavily.

"Steph, we're at a public beach. We can't do this here." Regretfully, he reached down and pulled her top back into place, thankful that his body had shielded hers from any prying eyes. He glanced up again at her face. She was grinning mischievously at him now.

"Did I get rid of the tense muscles in your back?"

"Yeah, but you replaced it with a different kind of tension in a different location."

"I can help with that, too." She blushed even as the daring words left her lips.

"I'm sure you can and later on I might even let you, but right now..." He stood and scooped her up into his arms and began to walk across the sand. "Right now, we both have to cool off."

"Jake, you wouldn't dare. Would you?"

"Sure I would." He leered at her evilly before tossing her into the water. She screeched and thrashed about trying to gain her footing before grabbing his legs and knocking him down into the water, too. Sputtering, he surfaced and lunged at her, but she slipped away, circling around him and launching a rear attack. After that, it was an all-out war that eventually left them laughing, exhausted and shivering from the extended exposure to the cool water. Running up to their spot on the beach, they sat huddled together, wrapped in towels while they warmed up.

Jake saw a family some distance away, setting out a picnic lunch. "Are you hungry?"

Her stomach chose that minute to rumble and she giggled. "There's your answer."

"There's a hotdog vendor over near the changing rooms. Do you want one?"

"Sure, with everything."

He quirked his eye brow at her. "Even onions?"

"I will, if you will."

He laughed, enjoying this playful side of her. "Okay, two hotdogs with everything coming up. I'll be right back." Grabbing some money from his wallet, he went to get their food.

As he stood in line, he watched Stephanie waiting for him on the blanket. She seemed to be looking at something. Squinting, he stared hard and then swore under his breath. Damn! He'd left his wallet sitting out. Rapidly, he inventoried the contents. Was there anything incriminating in there? He didn't think so but even so, his nerves tensed as he collected their meal and made his way to where she was sitting.

"Dinner is served," he announced. He schooled his voice to sound cheerful while scanning her face for any signs of distress. She seemed fine. Maybe he was overreacting. Casually, he reached for his wallet. "There it is. I'm glad I didn't lose it in the sand."

"I saw it on the edge of the towel and didn't want it to get buried. I hope you don't mind; I flipped through it."

"Find anything interesting?' He took a bite of the hotdog, keeping his face neutral, while his eyes watched her carefully.

"Not really." She licked some relish off her hand. "A driver's license, some credit cards. No pictures of old girl friends. Basically boring." She wrinkled her nose at him and grinned.

"Yeah that's me; a regular, boring guy." Inwardly breathing a sigh of relief, he chewed on his food while wondering what she'd say when she learned the truth.

Chapter 13

The day at the beach had been perfect, Stephanie thought to herself as she sat in the passenger seat of Jake's car. They'd had a wonderful time playing in the water, eating hotdogs and ice cream, even building sand castles. She had felt so at ease with Jake, like she'd known him all her life.

She stretched and relaxed against the headrest, a smile playing over her face as she contemplated the day. Walking along the edge of the beach, the water swirling about her ankles, she'd leaned against Jake and concentrated on the rhythm of his leg brushing against hers. He'd slung his arm around her shoulders, his fingers idly caressing her skin.

Everything about Jake felt so right. When she was with him, a part of her she'd never known existed seemed to come alive. Around him, she was playful and daring, boldly teasing him because somehow she knew deep inside that she really was safe with him; he'd never hurt her. She didn't understand the change that was coming over her, but she was sure this had to have been the best day of her life and she was reluctant to see it end.

Rolling her head to the side, she studied him. The sun was low in the sky but there was still enough light that she could see him clearly. His jaw was firm, his nose straight. His dark hair was slightly windblown giving him a casual appearance and the sun was turning his skin a golden brown. When he turned to glance her way, his blue eyes sparkled with intelligence and laughter and—dare she say it—love.

"Do we need to stop by your place for anything before heading home?"

Home.

She smiled, liking the sound of the word. It pleased her that he'd just assumed she would stay with him. It made her feel wanted, like they really belonged together.

"I need to pick up some clothes for work tomorrow and some food for Coco. I'm late feeding her as it is and if I don't come bearing gifts, there'll be no end to the meowing and complaining."

"She does have her own way of making her needs known, doesn't she?"

"That's putting it politely." She yawned, the fresh air having made her tired. "I think, having grown up on the streets, Coco's taken a vow, sort of like Scarlett O'Hara in 'Gone with the Wind'. Her motto is 'I'll never be hungry again'. Don't come between her and her food!

"She does look a bit chunky or maybe it's just all fur."

"It's a bit of both." The mention of fur reminded her of her allergy. "I have to grab my allergy pills. I forgot them again today."

Jake glanced at her. "Steph, have you sneezed or sniffled at all today?"

She reflected back and then shook her head. "Now that you mention it, no, I haven't."

"It's like I told you. You don't need those pills. It was just a summer cold, and now it's gone."

"I feel fine today, so maybe you're right. I hope so, because I didn't like the side effects of them; my brain was all muzzy, and I felt sort of paranoid."

He reached over, took her hand and held it against his thigh. "Steph, believe me. I know what I'm talking about. Forget the pills. I'll take care of you."

She liked the sound of that, 'I'll take care of you'. It was like he really cared and planned to be around for quite awhile. It made her feel all warm and fuzzy inside, and she spent the rest of the ride to her house contemplating what it might be like to have a future with him.

As they drove down her street, the headlights from Jake's car cut a swath through the darkness. The sun had set and, as usual, her neighbourhood was quiet. A few cars were parked on the road, but for the most part the street was empty. Some houses had lights on, and Mr. Hardy's dog gave a half-hearted woof in response to the sound of Jake's car. A typical night in the sleepy suburbs.

Stephanie climbed out of the vehicle, and walked up to the house fumbling in her purse for her keys. Jake gathered the newspaper from the front lawn, while she unlocked the door. It swung open and she started to step inside, but then paused. Something seemed wrong. An uneasy feeling was sweeping over her again, like someone was watching and she turned quickly to scan up and down the road, searching for the source.

"What's the matter, Steph?" Jake spoke from beside her and she jumped, so absorbed in looking for the source of her unease that she'd temporarily forgotten he was there.

She rubbed her hands up and down her arms trying to ease the goose bumps that had sprung up. "I don't know. I'm having that feeling again, like someone is watching me."

"Do you think he's been back?" Jake put his arm protectively around her shoulders while glancing around the front yard. "Maybe I should go in first, just in case."

"No. It's my home. I won't let someone make me afraid of my own house." After one last glance up and down the road, she took a deep breath and stepped inside, recalling her earlier vow to not be a victim.

She stood in the living room looking around. Everything seemed the same. Her library books were on the floor by the sofa. The cushions were slightly askew and showed traces of cat hair. Mail sat neatly stacked on the entryway table. Nothing obvious had been disturbed, yet the shadows in the corners and the darkness of the hallway leading to her bedroom made her wary.

Jake moved to stand beside her and she leaned into the warmth of his body.

"It's funny. It didn't bother me earlier today when I came to get my bathing suit. I just ran in and out without even thinking, but something about the dark makes everything more sinister."

He gave her a comforting hug. "The dark doesn't actually exist, you know. It's just an absence of light." She looked at him quizzically and he chuckled. "Really. I'm not making it up. It's an actual scientific fact."

He appeared so serious that she couldn't help but shake her head and laugh. "If you say so."

She made herself walk farther into the room, looking around, adjusting a picture here, a vase there. It was still the same cozy home. Nothing had changed. She was just letting her imagination get the best of her.

Taking a deep breath, she forced herself to relax. Enough dithering. She pasted a smile on her face and tried to speak confidently. "I'll just gather up a few things that I need from my bedroom. Could you get some cat food for Coco? It's in the kitchen. Look in the bottom cupboard, the one nearest the back door."

Jake studied her for a moment, perhaps trying to decide if she was really okay or not. Finally he nodded. "It's a difficult job, but I'll do my best to carry it out." Mockingly, he saluted her and she stuck her tongue out at him before heading off to the bedroom. His silliness helped her relax and she entered her room without a care.

Digging through her closet, she found some clothes to wear for work and a travel bag to put them in. Fresh underwear, a few pieces of jewellery and she was set to go. After turning off the light, she headed to the kitchen.

"Jake, did you find the cat food?" She called out to him as she walked down the hallway. When he didn't answer, she called out his name again. "Jake?"

A little spark of fear sprang to life inside her. He had to have heard her, the house wasn't that big. She quickened her steps. "Jake?" Stepping into the kitchen, she found him standing with his back to her. "Jake, why didn't you answer?"

He turned to look at her, his brow furrowed, his jaw tightly clenched.

"You've had a visitor."

She glanced in the direction he indicated and gasped. Scrawled on her fridge in dark red was a message: I'm watching you Stephanie—JS.

"Oh no! Oh no! Not again." She backed out of the room, her breath coming in short panicked pants.

Jake followed her and grabbed her shoulders. "Steph, look at me. Calm down!"

She dragged her gaze away from the fridge and looked at him. Everything seemed blurry except for his intense blue eyes.

"You're going to hyperventilate. Breathe slowly and deeply." He led her to the couch and put his hand on her stomach. "Breathe deep, down here, in your belly. Watch my hand and make it move when you breathe. That's it. Slowly. Deeply."

Stephanie listened to the sound of his voice and tried to follow his instructions. The rush of fear began to subside. Jake was with her; she was safe. After a few moments, she felt more in control and looked up at him. "Thanks. Sorry to freak out like that. The message—it's in red. Is it…?" She couldn't make herself say the word.

"Blood? No." He reached out and brushed her hair from her face, his touch tender and soothing. "I don't think so. It smells like ketchup to me. Do you want to call the police or shall I?"

"It's my house, my problem. I'll call."

As they sat waiting for the police, he held her close. "You know, Steph. We're creating our own little tradition here."

"What's that?"

"Most people end a date with a kiss at the door or coffee and some snuggling. But not us. We get together with the police."

Steph leaned back and gave him a mock scowl. "You have a really weird sense of humour, do you know that, St. Clair?"

"It's one of my many charms." He gave her a crooked smile.

The police appeared yet again, and checked for fingerprints on the fridge and within the message itself. Ketchup was confirmed as the substance used to write the words. For some reason, they asked to talk to her alone, while another officer questioned Jake outside.

"If you don't mind ma'am, leave the message on the fridge until we double check with the boys in the crime lab. I've taken several pictures of it and gathered a sample, but they might want something else." Officer Carter, the same policeman who'd taken her statement when the shop had been broken in to, was on the job again.

"Sure. I don't care about the cleanliness of my kitchen right now. I just want this person caught."

"Very understandable, Miss Fields. Do you have any idea of who JS is?"

She shook her head. "Not really. The only person I can think of with those initials is Jarrod Simpson. I talked to you about him this morning, but that happened years ago so I really doubt it's him again."

"I pulled the record of that incident and we will go over that file again, just in case. Now, what about your boyfriend?"

"Jake? What about him?"

"His initials are JS." He raised a brow and looked at her expectantly.

"Really?

"Jake St. Clair – JS."

She frowned and replied slowly. "You know I hadn't even thought about that. Strange coincidence, I guess."

"Uh-huh." He gave her a doubtful look. "When were you last in the house?"

"This afternoon. Jake and I were going to the beach. We stopped by so I could get my bathing suit."

"And did either of you go into the kitchen?"

"No. Well at least I didn't. I went into my bedroom and put on my bathing suit. Jake waited in the living room for me."

"And how long was that?"

"Umm—about fifteen or twenty minutes, I think."

"Fifteen or twenty minutes to put on a bathing suit?"

"Well... I had to shave my legs." She ducked her head, a bit embarrassed at having to share the fact. It wasn't any of his business that she'd shaved a bit elsewhere as well.

Her admission didn't even cause a flicker of expression on the officer's face. "And what was Mr. St. Clair doing during that time?"

"Waiting."

"Just standing and waiting?"

"Well, he might have sat down or looked out the window. I don't know. I didn't ask him. What are you trying to imply?" She looked at the officer with narrowed eyes, an uneasy feeling rising in her as to the direction his questions were taking.

"Nothing, Miss Fields. Just confirming what happened. So you didn't enter the kitchen."

"No, sir."

"Did Mr. St. Clair go into the kitchen?"

"No. At least I don't think so. He might have. We didn't really talk about it." She began to twist her fingers nervously.

"So the message could have been written anytime between when you left last night and when you came back this evening."

She nodded.

"Besides when you were changing, has Mr. St. Clair been with you all the time since last night?"

"Yes. Except when he went to get some bread this morning."

"And how long was he gone?"

"I'm not sure, maybe a little over half an hour, forty-five minutes tops."

"A long time to get bread, wouldn't you say?"

"Look, Jake is my boyfriend. He has nothing to do with this message and I really don't like you asking all these questions." Stephanie could feel tears rising in her eyes, though she wasn't sure if it was fear, frustration or sheer temper.

The officer closed his notebook. "Sorry to upset you, ma'am. I'm just doing my job. Will you still be at Mr. St. Clair's tonight?"

"Yes."

"And tomorrow?"

"I have to go to work tomorrow so if you need me during the day, I'll be at my store, Fields of Flowers. You have the number." She answered tightly, thoroughly annoyed with the man.

"Thank you, ma'am. Once again, I'm sorry for upsetting you." He turned to go, and then paused. "It looks like our thief is turning into a stalker. These types are usually all talk and no action, but do watch out. Try not to go anywhere alone. I'd hate to see anything happen to you."

"Me, too." She responded softly, wrapping her arms around herself and staring out the window to where another officer was questioning Jake in the front yard. This was just ridiculous. There was some crazy guy out there, and they were worrying about Jake having the same initials and taking too long to get the bread. Jake was her boyfriend. He'd never do anything to hurt her.

"Officer?"

"Yes ma'am?"

"Why would someone leave their initials? Isn't that implicating themselves? Making it easier for you guys to catch them?"

"Possibly. Sometimes these people like to taunt the authorities. They leave clues and then laugh, thinking that they're more clever than the police. Other times, they want to get caught, or they might even leave false evidence just to confuse us."

"So JS might be the person's initials or it might be a false lead."

"That's correct." He gestured towards the front yard. "It looks like they're done with Mr. St. Clair. You're free to go, but like I said, be careful."

Trying to keep her dislike of him in perspective, she gave the man a vague smile. He *was* just doing his job, but his suggestions about Jake were both ludicrous and irritating. She went to greet Jake who was just coming in the front door. He looked worried and she gave him a hug. "Are you all right?"

"Yeah—I don't like the direction some of their questions are taking though."

"Me either." She looked up at him, trying to let her belief in him show through her eyes. "I know you have nothing to do with this."

He stared at her for a moment, and then gently brushed the back of his fingers over her cheek. "Thanks. It means a lot to me, knowing that you trust me."

"Of course I trust you." She placed her hand over his heart. "You're not some weirdo who stalks women just for kicks."

"No, I definitely wouldn't stalk you just for kicks."

"I know." She gave him another hug. "The police are packing up. I'll just lock the doors and then we can leave. I really don't want to stay here any longer than I have to."

"Okay. I'll just grab Coco's food. I never did get around to collecting it."

"Little wonder after finding that message."

"Yeah." He seemed distracted, but she put it down to concern for her and went to pick up the tote containing clothes. It would be good to get back to Jake's. She felt safe there.

Chapter 14

Jake opened a can of cat food and fed Coco, while Stephanie was in the shower removing traces of the beach. The cat wound around his ankles and purred in gratitude causing him to laugh at its antics. "See? We didn't abandon you. There was just a delay."

Coco butted her head against his hand before diving into the meal. He watched the cat eat for a moment then rinsed the can and put it in the recycling bin. Leaning against the counter, he listened to the sounds of the shower and rubbed his hands over his face.

This was getting complicated. The police were asking questions that they shouldn't be, casting doubts on him just as Stephanie was showing signs of being ready to move on to the next level. He didn't want it to be this way. She was supposed to come to him with no reservations. Perhaps it was just a silly fantasy that he had, but he'd planned this for so long.

In his mind, he played out the scene. They'd be somewhere romantic and intimate, with candles casting a warm glow over the room and soft music in the background. Stephanie would look up at him, her eyes full of trust and hot with desire. Sliding her hands over his chest and around his neck, she'd pull him close for a deep, passionate kiss that would leave no doubt in his mind as to how she felt. Then, in a voice trembling with need, she'd assure him that she understood about the past—his, hers…theirs—and that she wanted a future with him. But most important of all, she'd declare her unconditional love and acceptance. That was when he'd…

A sharp pain shot through his leg and he was jerked back into reality. Looking down, Jake saw that Coco had finished her meal and was trying to use his leg as a scratching post. Disengaging her claws, he sent her on her way, wincing slightly as she immediately headed for the corner of the sofa and resumed doing her nails. Adding 'scratching post' to the shopping list on the fridge door, he rinsed the cat's dish and put it away.

The sound of the shower running stopped and, after a few moments, Stephanie wandered out, wrapped in a towel. "Jake? Do you have anything for a burn? I guess the sunscreen wore off when we were playing in the water." She was twisting her neck looking at her shoulders and trying to see her back. The flesh was decidedly pink.

"Ouch! That looks sore."

"Yeah, it is a bit."

Reaching out to touch her, he paused and then thought better of it. "Just a minute; let me check the medicine cabinet." He went into the bathroom and looked around. There was some lotion—a travel pack from a motel. It would have to do. He squeezed some on his hands and turned to find Stephanie entering the bathroom.

"Did you find anything?"

"Let's try this. Turn around and I'll rub it in."

She followed his directions but cautioned him at the same time. "Be careful, it's really tender."

"I will be—don't worry." He gently ran his hands over her shoulders, closing his eyes and concentrating on the heat radiating from her skin.

"Ooh, that feels good. It's like the burn's just disappearing."

'Yes." He cleared his throat and stared at her back. The pink had faded away and her skin was just lightly tanned now. "It's a fast acting remedy. I can do the rest of you too, if you'd like."

She turned. "Sure, my arms are a bit pink. Feel free."

He rubbed his hands up and down her arms and then across the part of her chest that was above the towel. Her eyes drifted shut as he stroked her skin. "Mmm. Nice touch, St. Clair."

His fingers skimmed along the edge of the towel. Having her so close was playing havoc with his self-control. He took a deep steadying breath. "Are you sunburnt anywhere else?"

"Why don't you check and see?" She opened her eyes and watched his face as she loosened the towel and let it fall to the floor.

He drew in a quick breath as he took in her naked body; her gently rounded breasts tipped with pink, her slim waist, the golden curls at the apex of her thighs. Looking up at her, he noted her nervously biting her lip and the faint flush on her cheeks.

"You're beautiful, Steph, so beautiful." Slowly he reached out and skimmed his hands down her body to her hips. Pulling her closer, he wrapped his arms around her and kissed her softly. This wasn't his perfect fantasy, but the warm steamy air from the shower came a close second to candlelight and music. "Are you sure? Is this what you really want?" He murmured the words against her lips.

She nodded shyly, her fingers tracing a pattern across his chest. "Yes. Today, with you, everything was perfect, and this is how I want the day to end. I want to be with you, Jake. I want us to be together. But I...I've never done this before and, I'm not sure what to do."

"I know." He kissed her softly. "Don't worry. It will come to you naturally. It's instinct." Kissing her again, he ran his hands up and down her back.

Returning his kisses, she cupped his face in her hands, pressing herself closer to him. The heat of her body penetrated through his clothing and he groaned against her mouth. She was right. The day had been perfect, but then, at her house...

His brain was trying to point out why this wasn't a good idea, but reason was rapidly melting as the flames of desire grew within him. Pulling away for a breath, he shook his head slightly to try to clear away the haze that was fogging his thinking, but Stephanie raked her fingers down his spine to clutch his buttocks and he was lost. Bending, he swept her up into his arms and carried her to the bedroom. Stephanie was his again.

Hours later, he climbed out of bed, careful not to wake the woman sleeping beside him. He stood staring down at her tousled hair and flushed face. The covers were tangled about her legs and her upper torso was bare, still showing faint signs of the passion they'd shared. Without a word, he left the room, quietly closing the door behind him.

Her cat was sleeping on the sofa and blinked at him before obviously deciding he was unimportant and resuming its nap. The clock on the wall ticked softly in the background, and the light of the moon shot a beam of silver across the floor. He followed the path of light, padding across the carpet and out onto the balcony. The night air was warm on his naked body and he stood, hands braced on the railing with his face tipped up to the heavens.

Tonight it had been completed. Destiny. Fate. The will of the gods. Whatever you wanted to call it, she was his now. There'd be no going back, he knew her too well. Having freely given herself to him, she would stay with him now for the rest of her life.

'Barring any great tragedy,' a nasty voice whispered. *'If the police arrest you as the stalker, then what?'* The wind stirred and the leaves rustled, like voices in the night.

He gripped the railing.

No.

He wouldn't listen.

It was too late to change his mind. This was where he wanted to be, what he wanted to be. Staring up at the stars, he felt their pull. The voices called to him, pulled at something deep and elemental inside him. Something he could hardly control. Clenching his jaw, he tried to resist.

Chapter 15

Stephanie stretched and rolled over, reaching for Jake. Her hand moved across the mattress finding only the coolness of cotton. She opened one bleary eye and noted that the spot beside her was empty. A little wave of disappointment washed over her and she felt something akin to a pout forming on her lips. Waking up by herself wasn't how she'd envisioned the morning after.

Maybe he was just in the bathroom. She stretched, wincing slightly as stiff muscles protested. A smile spread over her face and she ran her hand down her body. It didn't feel different, but it was. Now, it belonged to Jake. She blushed as memories of the previous night ran through her mind. The things he'd done to her with his hands and mouth! She'd never known... And the things she'd done to him! But it had all felt right and natural. Like Jake had said, it was instinct.

Dreamily, she relived bits and pieces of the night before, how she'd awoke in the early hours and brazenly run her hands over his body. With a shiver, she recalled his mouth skimming over her shoulder, to her breasts and then lower still…

Already her body was craving his again and she moved restlessly, wishing he was there with her. She frowned wondering why he still hadn't returned.

Cocking her head, she listened carefully and realized that she was alone in the apartment. He was out somewhere. Getting more groceries? Possibly. Oh well, it didn't matter; there'd be no repeat of last night now. Rolling out of bed, she padded to the bathroom.

As she waited for the water to warm up, she studied herself in the mirror. Light tan lines from her bathing suit could be seen. That's strange, she thought. There was no evidence of yesterday's sunburn. Last night, after her shower, she'd been decidedly pink. With her fair colouring, it had happened to her numerous times before. Her skin should still be pink and tender, not tanned. What type of cream had Jake used? She'd have to stock up on it, whatever it was. Looking on the counter, she saw no tube or bottle but then remembered it had been in a small foil pouch. Pulling the garbage pail forward, she peered inside and took out the lone item.

It was a package of hand cream from a motel chain. The brand was a common one she'd used before and there was no way it would cure sunburn. She stood and stared at her shoulders, then turned to look over her shoulder at her back. Definitely no sunburn there, either; just a tan. Had she imagined it? No. She distinctly recalled the heat generating off her skin, the tender to the touch feeling. Frowning, she stepped into the shower and began to wash, puzzling over her missing burn.

By the time she was done showering, she still didn't have an answer and was determined to ask Jake about her mysterious cure when he returned, but after dressing, she checked the clock and realized it was almost time to leave for work. She was just debating about leaving him a note, when he walked in. He was dressed casually in jeans and a short-sleeved blue shirt that accented the blue of his eyes. His black hair was slightly windblown and a wide smile spread across his face when he saw her.

"Hi!" He walked up to her and kissed her warmly. "Almost ready to leave for work?"

"Yeah, I was just going to leave you a note and call a cab."

"No need. I brought your car over here." He dropped the keys into her hand.

"Really?"

"I hope you don't mind. I got your keys from your purse and took a cab to the house, then drove back here. I figured you'd want your own transportation today."

"Thanks, Jake." She smiled up at him. "That was really thoughtful of you."

"Hey—that's the kind of guy I am." He pulled her into a hug and gave her a longer, more intense kiss. She felt her toes curling and wished she didn't have to go to work. Slowly, reluctantly, they broke apart. Jake gently twined a strand of her hair around his finger. "How are you feeling this morning?"

She felt her face getting warm, but bravely met his gaze. "I'm fine. Great, actually. Thank you for making last night so perfect."

"My pleasure." His eyes twinkled, then he bent and nuzzled the sensitive spot just behind her ear. She let her head fall to the side giving him better access. A shiver ran down her spine as his teeth grazed her skin. Her tanned skin. The skin with no sunburn.

"Jake?"

"Hmm?"

"What happened to my sunburn?" She felt him still momentarily, then move to brushing his lips along her jaw line.

"Your sunburn? I put some cream on it, remember?"

"Yes, but it was just ordinary hand cream; I saw the package in the garbage this morning." She pulled back and looked him in the eye. "My sunburn's totally gone and that's never happened before. I burn easily and it lasts for days. Jake, what happened?"

He stepped away and picked up Coco, who was lounging on the coffee table. "I have the healing touch, I guess." Jake spoke lightly, walking towards the balcony, keeping his back to her.

"That's not an answer."

Slowly he turned around, as if reluctant to face her. "Look, we can talk about this when you get home, tonight. I have something important to tell you and there isn't enough time to do it properly right now. You're going to be late for work. It takes longer to drive to the shop from here, than it does from your house."

Stephanie studied him for a moment before shrugging. It really wasn't important enough to start an argument over, she decided. "All right, we'll talk tonight." She noted that Jake appeared relieved. He tucked Coco under one arm and walked her to the door.

"I want you to be extra careful today. The police said it's highly unlikely that this stalker person will do anything beyond verbal threats, but don't take any chances." He gripped her chin lightly and stared right into her eyes. "Don't go anywhere by yourself. Let Paula make the deliveries. I'll call the store in about half an hour to make sure you've arrived safely."

"Yes, Mother." She mocked before giving him a quick peck and closing the door. Humming quietly to herself, she walked to the parking lot, thinking how nice it was to have someone to kiss goodbye. Looking up towards Jake's apartment, she saw him watching her from the balcony. 'That's so sweet,' she thought to herself as she waved at him. 'He's making sure I get to my car safely.' With another jaunty wave, she climbed inside and drove off, already counting the hours until she would see him again.

Paula was full of questions about Stephanie's weekend, both excited that her friend had spent the past two days with Jake, and scared that someone seemed to be stalking her. They talked about the incident as they prepared the day's special orders.

"And he left a message written in ketchup on the fridge door?"

"Yeah. At first I thought it was blood. It really scared me." She shivered at the memory.

"Good thing Jake was there."

"Uh huh, but the police were really weird." She paused in the middle of inserting some baby's breath into a bouquet. "They kept asking questions about Jake and sort of implying that he could be the stalker."

"Well that's ridiculous. The man is head over heels for you, and you are for him. Why would he need to stalk you?" Paula snorted and shook her head.

"My feelings exactly. The police officer kept saying he was just doing his job, and I suppose they have to rule out every possibility, but it just bugged me." Stephanie poked a bow into the arrangement with more force than strictly necessary. "Here I am. I finally have this great guy who is interested in me and they're trying to turn him into a criminal." Stephanie took a deep calming breath and carried the arrangement to the refrigerated display case where it would stay cool until delivery time. "So, how was your weekend? Is Chelsea still feeling okay?"

"Yep, the kiddo is fine. It was just a little tummy virus that she picked up. But guess what? I met a new guy this weekend."

"Really? Why doesn't that surprise me?" Stephanie grinned at her friend. "You only broke up with Kevin last weekend."

"Yeah, I went a whole week without a date." Paula sighed dramatically.

"It constantly amazes me that in a town this size you can find so many eligible men to date, yet I had to wait for one to move in from out of town."

"Well Jack is actually from out of town too. He's been subletting an apartment for the past month—he's a product rep for a software company and they're blitzing the area. With any luck, he'll be in town for another couple of weeks."

"Oh—so it's going to be a long term relationship this time? A whole two weeks?"

"Stephanie!" Paula threw some floral foam at her friend. "Good thing I know you're just kidding."

"I am." Stephanie gave her friend a quick hug before getting out a vase for the next arrangement on the list. "I just worry about you sometimes. How did you meet him?"

"He was standing outside the shop when I left Saturday night. I literally ran into him and he picked up my purse for me. One thing led to another..." Paula had a Cheshire like grin on her face. Stephanie had to laugh. She'd seen her friend in action before. The poor man probably didn't even know what had hit him. Paula was an expert in the game of love. Hmm... Perhaps she was the one to ask.

"Paula, can I ask you a question?"

"Sure. It sounds serious."

"It is, kind of." She leaned a hip against the counter and studied her friend carefully. "How do you know when you're in love?"

"In love? You're asking me?" Paula looked up in surprise. "The woman who goes through men faster than we go through flowers?"

Stephanie shrugged. "I don't know who else to ask. Have you ever been in love? Really, really in love?"

Paula twirled the carnation that she was stripping leaves from and got a bit dreamy eyed. "Once, with Chelsea's father. At least I was in love; I guess he wasn't. Dirty cheating bastard." She snapped the flower's stem. "Oops!"

Stephanie took the flower from her friend and trimmed the end neatly. "So how did you feel about him? Before he became a dirty cheating bastard, that is."

"I loved him. I couldn't wait to see him and talk to him, or just be with him." She shrugged. "The sex was great, but we had fun too. Sometimes we just sat quietly together or we'd talk about crazy stuff like if marshmallows were better toasted or plain. We'd laugh and argue and then make up." A reminiscent look came over her face. "I thought he was wonderful, smart, funny. And he always seemed concerned about me."

"So what happened?" She asked softly, almost hating to bring up what must have surely been a painful experience.

"I don't know. Chelsea was born. There was no money. We never had time for each other. Maybe he just couldn't handle the stress of a baby. He left when she was only a month old." Paula sniffed and looked around for a tissue. "Silly of me, isn't' it? Getting teary-eyed over that jerk, after all this time."

"Not silly at all." She squeezed her friend's hand. "Thanks for sharing."

"So, did it help? Do you think you're in love with Jake?" Paula finished wiping her eyes and threw the tissue away.

"Yeah, I think I am."

"And is he in love with you?"

"I think so. I hope so. He hasn't said it yet, but he acts like he is. Just before I left this morning, he said we'd have to talk about something important tonight and he was acting a bit strange." She decided not to tell Paula about the mysterious case of the disappearing sunburn. After all, it could have just been one of those strange, inexplicable occurrences.

"That could be it, then. Guys get all weird when it comes to using the big 'L' word. I can't wait until tomorrow morning to find out what happened." Paula grinned, her melancholia short-lived.

"I could call you at home and give you the scoop." Stephanie teased.

"No! Don't do that. Jack's coming over for supper and you never know where it might lead."

"Paula! You just met the man." She threw a flower at her in mock chastisement.

"Hey, if I can't have true love, I'll take the next best thing."

Stephanie shook her head and went to deal with a customer who had just walked in. Paula was her best friend, but she couldn't understand her casual attitude towards sex and her willingness to continually flit from one short term relationship to another, even when she knew there was little chance for a future. For herself, Stephanie wanted something permanent and stable; something that would last a lifetime. With Jake, she thought she might have found that. She really could picture herself spending the rest of her life by his side. Hopefully, Jake felt the same way too.

Chapter 16

He sat in his car, watching the customers entering and exiting the shop. They were both in there, but he couldn't make a move until the coast was clear. There were deliveries that had to be made; he'd placed one of them himself, just to be sure. One of them would have to leave to deliver it; he wondered which one. Not that it mattered. Either way would work. He could follow the car and grab her when she made the delivery at his apartment or, if she was the one that stayed behind, he could sneak into the shop through the back entrance. The silly woman hadn't even changed the lock. That door could be opened in under a minute.

Everything was going perfectly. It was time to carry out the final stage of his plan. Reaching under the seat, he pulled out the knife and fingered the blade. He nicked his thumb and watched the red fluid well up before sucking on it. It was warm and salty in his mouth. Chuckling to himself, he thought of the message he'd left on the fridge. Using ketchup had been inspired. He'd known that she'd think it was blood. And the initials, well, she needed a clue to get her thinking about him. Worrying. The tension and nervousness would be building inside her now. He'd be able to see it in her eyes and hear it in her voice. Fear was like an aphrodisiac to him.

'Next time it won't be ketchup,' he muttered to himself. 'It will be the real thing and I'll use your very own blood to write the words.' The thought excited him even more and he shifted uncomfortably in his seat.

Today. It had to be today. He couldn't wait any longer to hear her beg.

Sheathing the knife, he gripped the steering wheel. Come on, hurry up. Make the stupid deliveries. He glanced in the rear-view mirror and saw a police car pulling up. Slowly he ducked down in the car and watched in frustration as an officer walked into the flower shop. Damn. It was too dangerous. He couldn't stay here. What if one of them looked out and saw him while the police were in there?

Sitting up, he started the car and then carefully pulled away from the curb, making sure he drew no attention to himself. His jaw clenched in anger. Now he'd have to wait until tomorrow. He was a patient man, but this was lasting too long.

Taking deep breaths, he forced himself to stay calm. He'd take a drive. Find someplace quiet. Reassess his plan. Planning was everything. It had kept him from being caught all this time. It would work again. And if not, well, he'd seize whatever opportunity came along.

~~~

Stephanie glanced up from the order pad she was writing on. The bell for the front door usually signalled the entrance of a customer, but this time it was Officer Carter. She put down her pen and sat up straight, waiting for him to come to her. There were no customers in the store and Paula was eating her lunch out back. It was ironic that just when she was hoping to make up the shortfall from the money lost in the robbery, there was a lull in flower sales. Go figure.

"Good afternoon, Miss Fields."

"Officer Carter, how can I help you?"

"I just have a few more questions for you about the incidents that have taken place over the past few days. Do you have a minute?"

"Umm. Sure. My assistant is out back eating her lunch, but she can deal with any customers that might come in. Just let me tell her." Stephanie slipped into the back room to inform Paula and then returned. She settled on the stool behind the counter and folded her hands in her lap, prepared to be calm and polite no matter what ridiculous insinuations the man made. "What types of questions?"

"How long have you known Mr. St. Clair?"

"Jake? Well, I met him last Thursday so that was five days ago."

"And how did you meet?"
~~~

"He came into the store and startled me by accident. I spilled my coffee and dropped my bagel. Jake took me to the donut shop a few doors down to make up for ruining my lunch."

"And why did he come into this store in the first place?"

"To buy some flowers. This is a flower shop after all." She bit her lip to hold back the 'duh' she so badly wanted to add. Being sarcastic wasn't a good idea. The police, while obviously misguided, were on her side.

The officer raised his brows but just continued his line of questioning. "Do you know who the flowers were for?"

"Yes." She smiled at the memory. "They were for me."

"For you?" He raised a brow. "But you said he'd just met you when he came into the store. Why would he come into a store to buy flowers for a woman he hadn't met yet?"

She felt her cheeks growing warm as she explained. "Well, it's sort of silly, but apparently he saw me and wanted to meet me, so he came into the shop on Wednesday and asked Paula, my assistant, about me. Then he came in the next day to actually talk to me."

"And you didn't find that strange?"

"Strange? How so?"

"I mean, do you often have men asking about you and buying you bouquets when they haven't even met you?"

"No. Of course that doesn't happen all the time. Jake was just…well…he was just being nice. Romantic." She clenched her hands in her lap and tried to keep her indignation from showing in her voice. "There was nothing wrong with what he did. And I know he isn't the person stalking me."

"And how can you be so sure?"

"Because he already has me! I mean, I see him all the time, any time he wants. There's no reason for him to stalk me or leave creepy messages on my refrigerator."

"You're probably right, ma'am, but we're just trying to check all the angles. It just strikes us as curious that since you've met him, there's been an incident each day." He looked up from the notes he was making. "And the rash of break-ins across the town began just about the time that Mr. St. Clair moved here."

"They're all just coincidences. They do happen, you know." Stephanie could feel her temper rising and knew she was losing the battle to remain calm. What had happened to her usually placid personality? "Instead of worrying about Jake, you should be out there looking for real criminals. What about Jarrod Simpson? Have you found him yet?"

"Not quite. We know he was last seen in Bellingham, a small town about three hundred miles from here. He'd been in a severe accident and hospitalized for quite a while. Afterwards, he had to undergo reconstructive surgery. Unfortunately, because of the surgery, we no longer have a clear picture of what he looks like." As he spoke he was surveying the shop with his gaze, studying the windows, the door, the curtain to the back room before finally looking at Stephanie again. "All we know is that he's still tall and of average build with blue eyes and black hair, but that's the only sure thing we have. No one's seen or heard from him in the past two years."

"So he could be right here in Weston and no one would know it was him."

"That's correct, Miss Fields."

Stephanie shivered at the thought. Jarrod Simpson could be anyone. He could have stood beside her in the grocery store or even been a customer in the shop and she wouldn't have known.

"We will have extra patrols going by this store until the stalker is found. Are you still staying at Mr. St. Clair's?" She nodded. "We'll have extra night patrols in that area as well then. As I said before, take care and be extra cautious. Try not to be alone if it can be helped."

"All right. Thanks for stopping by." I think, she whispered to herself. Now she really felt creeped out. Jarrod Simpson could be anyone, anywhere. He could be wearing coloured contacts and have dyed his hair. Suddenly, all she wanted to do was go home and be with Jake. She almost laughed. Going home now meant Jake's apartment. Somehow she doubted she would ever view her little house as 'home' again.

Paula came out of the back room. "I overheard. They really don't trust Jake do they?"

"Yeah and I can't figure out why. He gave me his references, his old employers, the bank manager, satisfied customers."

"Did you check them out?"

"Yes. Well, some. I did call the bank manager, but afterward I felt silly and I didn't check the rest."

"Maybe they're bogus?"

"Paula! How could you even think that?"

Her friend shrugged. "Just playing devil's advocate. I don't really think Jake is the stalker."

"Thank heavens or I'd have to look for a new best friend." She began to pace the length of the shop. "Listen, I really don't feel like working today. I kind of want to cocoon at home with Jake. What do you say, we make these three deliveries and close up early?"

"Close early? " Paula's eyebrows shot upward. "You are upset, aren't you?"

"Mondays are never that busy. I'll put a sign on the door asking people to come back tomorrow and I'll switch the answering machine on."

"That sounds like a plan." Paula grinned, obviously warming to the idea. "Woo hoo! A holiday! Not that I'm happy about the reason, but I never look a gift horse in the mouth."

Paula made up a sign and Stephanie turned on the answering machine. When Paula offered to make the deliveries, Steph let her. She was too anxious to get home to worry about taking advantage of her friend's goodwill.

Jake wasn't home when she got back to the apartment. Thankfully, he'd given her a key so she could let herself in. Once inside she fussed with Coco, who was happy with the unexpected attention, then sat down to watch TV. Nothing caught her fancy so she turned it off and began to wander around the apartment.

Unsure of what to do with herself, her thoughts turned to work. Had she turned the answering machine on properly? She hardly ever used it and was always doing something wrong.

Deciding to check, she dug through her purse for the instructions and her password, then set them on the coffee table beside the phone. She sat down on the sofa and called the shop then waited for the message to play. It rang twice and her own voice came on.

"Hello, you've reached Fields of Flowers. I'm unavailable right now, but if you leave your name and number, I'll get back to you as soon as possible. Thanks and have a nice day."

She waited for the beep, and then left a message. "Hi! Just doing a test—hope this works."

After hanging up she redialled to check if the message had recorded and if she could retrieve it. Yep, there was her voice but... Oh another message had been recorded as well. Might as well listen and see what work awaited her tomorrow. She grabbed a pen and paper, just in case she wanted to jot something down.

A raspy voice came over the phone. "Stephanie, I know where you are and I'm coming for you soon. Next time the blood will be real."

Screaming, she jumped up and dropped the phone.

Waves of hot and cold washed over her. Her heart was pounding and she couldn't think, couldn't breathe. She gripped the back of a nearby chair. Be calm, be calm, she told herself. Breathe like Jake showed you.

Random thoughts ricocheted through her mind and she struggled to focus on even one of them. Oh God, he knew where she was! What was she going to do? She had to find Jake—but where was he? He hadn't said anything this morning about having to go anywhere. Looking frantically around the room, she wondered if there was a business card with his cell phone number. There was nothing in the living room, but maybe in the bedroom…?

Hurrying into the next room, she scanned the night table and pulled open the drawer. A gun was lying there. She froze and stared at it.

She hated guns, but lots of people had them for protection. Her hand hovered over it. Should she take it? No. She'd never even held a real gun, let alone used one. She'd probably shoot herself. But, once Jake was here, he'd know what to do with it.

Continuing her search, she checked on top of the dresser before starting to pull open drawers. Socks, underwear, T-shirts... Yes! There was large file folder. Maybe she'd find a letterhead with his number on it. She glanced at the label and then did a double take. Her name was on the top.

A strange feeling washed over her. With trembling hands she opened the file and randomly pulled out a page. Her own likeness stared back at her. Her knees felt weak and she sat down heavily on the edge of the bed and began to look through the file.

There was a copy of her birth certificate, the notice of her parents' death, her high school diploma... Flipping over more pages, she found a stack of photos, all of her, and all taken without her knowledge. Her hands started to shake and she could barely pick up the pictures. There she was at the grocery store, in the mall, walking down the street, unlocking her front door...

Pushing the file off her lap she back away from the incriminating evidence. Oh no, oh no. Jake was the stalker! This couldn't be happening to her. Not Jake. Please God, not Jake. She shook her head, tears streaming down her face. This couldn't be real. But it was. Why else would he have all these pictures of her?

Suddenly, she recalled the phone message and knew she had to get away before Jake returned, but where could she go? Paula's house was the only place she could think of. And what about Coco? She couldn't leave the cat here. What if he hurt the poor animal? And she had to tell the police.

Thought after thought flit through her mind in rapid succession and she began to race through the apartment.

She grabbed Coco and stuffed her into her pet crate then snatched up her purse. As fast as possible she hurried down the hallway and into the elevator. The floor numbers seemed to move by so slowly. Five... Four... Three... Two... Main floor.

Almost running across the lobby and parking lot, she headed for her car, the cat carrier bumping against her thigh and

Coco yowling in protest inside. Once in the car, she quickly pulled out of the parking lot and onto the street. Just as she was turning the corner, she saw Jake's car coming down the road.

"Please, please, please don't let him see me," she prayed. Taking the corner too quickly, Coco's pet crate slipped across the seat and another sad wail emitted from the cage. "I'm sorry baby, I'm sorry, but we have to get away." Fumbling in her purse, she found her cell phone and called the police.

"Hello? This is Stephanie Fields. Is Officer Carter in? No? Then can you give him this message? Tell him I called and there was another threatening message, this time on my answering machine at work. The stalker is Jake." She thought she'd choke on the words. Another turn was coming up and she was going too fast. She dropped the phone, needing both hands on the wheel to manoeuvre the corner. Glancing at the rear-view mirror, she didn't see anyone behind her. Possibly Jake hadn't noticed her car. Maybe she was safe, after all. A shiver swept over her—somehow she doubted that.

Chapter 17

Jake was heading for home both frustrated and excited. The frustration stemmed from the fact that several leads he'd been following had turned into dead ends. With all the experience he had in hiding information and creating bogus identities, he'd erroneously assumed his task would be easy. He'd been wrong, and it didn't sit well with him. His hands flexed on the steering wheel as his thoughts drifted to what had happened at Stephanie's house last night. The police had questioned him extensively. When people started questioning his background too much he got nervous. He'd never slipped up before, but there was always a chance... Pushing the problem from his mind, he decided to concentrate on a more pleasing topic.

On the back seat of the car, he had grocery bags filled with the necessary ingredients for a special meal. He was planning on telling Stephanie the whole truth tonight, and figured a nice dinner and a little wine couldn't hurt. It would be a shock. She'd protest, but he'd make her listen; he'd waited too long for this moment. There was no going back.

A car whizzed by, taking the corner too fast and he thought it looked like Steph's car, which was impossible, since she was at work. Unless she was making deliveries? No, he'd told her to stay in the store and let Paula do that. Perhaps Paula was using Steph's car. Geez, if that was how Paula drove, he was surprised any of the floral arrangements ever arrived in one piece. He pulled into his parking spot and headed inside.

Thomas, the doorman was just coming on duty.

"Afternoon, Thomas."

"Good afternoon, Mr. St. Clair. Been grocery shopping and to the wine store I see. A special night?"

"Yep. A special night and special meal for a special lady."

"If you mean Miss Fields, you just missed her."

"Stephanie was here?"

"It certainly looked like her. Mind you, I was just arriving. Whoever it was, they were almost running across the parking lot with a pet carrier. It sounded like a mighty upset cat was inside."

"Hmm. Thanks for the information, Thomas."

Jake frowned as he waited impatiently for the elevator and then hurried to the apartment. The door was wide open.

"Steph?" He walked inside, but immediately knew she wasn't there. It was too quiet. There was none of the energy in the air that always signalled her presence to him. Setting the groceries on the counter, he heard a faint beeping sound coming from the living room. It led him to the phone, which was lying on the floor. He picked it up and listened, but the connection had been broken.

Pressing the appropriate combination of buttons, he had the phone redial the last call made. The phone rang and Stephanie's voice sounded in his ear. She'd called the flower shop, but why? He picked up a card from the coffee table. It was the instructions on how to retrieve messages and her password was on it.

He hesitated, then decided to see what was on her voice mail that could have upset her so much. Maybe there would be a clue as to why she'd left or where she was going. An emergency involving Ella, perhaps? That would make sense.

As he listened, he wandered towards the bedroom. As soon as he stepped in the doorway, he froze. His file on her was scattered all over the bed and several pictures of her lay on the carpet looking up at him. How had she found it? What must she be thinking?

A male voice in his ear caught his attention. "Stephanie, I know where you are and I'm coming for you soon. Next time, the blood will be real."

"Shit!" He threw the phone down and raked his hands through his hair. Where could she have gone? She didn't have any family—just Ella McCreedy and Paula. Quickly, he sifted through his papers on her and found the two addresses.

~~~
~~~

Stephanie pulled into Paula's driveway and turned off the engine. Resting her forehead on the steering wheel, she tried to bring some semblance of order to her racing thoughts. Jake was the stalker and he was threatening to kill her. She still couldn't believe it. He was so kind, attentive, gentle. But the facts spoke for themselves. The break-in had occurred just after she'd met him; he'd actually been in the shop and had left on the pretext of running errands. Perhaps his plan had to been to attack her that very first night, but when she'd noticed that someone was at the rear door, he'd covered up his real intent by taking money from the till.

Her name tag was another bit of evidence. In the coffee shop, he'd commented on it and then suddenly it was gone. A real thief wouldn't have taken it; it had no worth except that by stealing it, she'd been hurt. The message on the fridge, well, he'd probably written it while she was changing and, of course, there was the all too damning file folder full of pictures of her. There could be no logical explanation for that except that he was stalking her.

'Oh Jake, why did it have to be you? Why are you doing this to me? I love you. I thought you loved me.' The words were whispered as she wrapped her arms around herself as if trying to ward off the pain of his betrayal. The past few days had all been a fantasy; part of an elaborate ruse to make her trust him. She should have known better. Why would any normal man be interested in a boringly ordinary person like her?

He'd probably seen her as an easy target for his sick game; a naive, lonely woman who'd be so taken up with his looks that she'd never question his motives. She'd fallen into his trap without even the slightest protest, giving him both her body and her heart, thinking he felt the same way. In actual fact, it was all just some twisted joke. He'd probably been laughing at her all along. The idea hurt unbearably.

Sniffling, she realized her face was wet. Grabbing a tissue, she wiped her eyes and blew her nose. This wasn't the time to fall apart. Taking a deep, shuddering breath, she tried to calm herself down. Once she was safe and Jake was behind bars, then she'd mourn the loss of the man she thought she knew. Right now, she needed to find a place to hide until he was caught.

It was only a matter of time before he found out where Paula lived, so staying here wasn't an option. She could leave Coco here though. Paula liked the beast, and Chelsea would be delighted to have a temporary playmate—how Coco would feel about that was another matter, but it couldn't be helped.

Gathering her purse, she noticed that her cell phone was on the floor of the car where she'd dropped it earlier. 'I never even finished my call to the police,' she realized. 'Once I drop Coco off and get on the road again, I'll call them again.' Leaving the phone where it lay, she climbed out of the car, grabbed Coco's pet shuttle from the back seat, and walked to the front door.

As Stephanie stood on the step waiting, she kept looking over her shoulder worrying that Jake would show up at any minute. She rang the bell again, twisting her purse strap in her hands and urging Paula to hurry. Finally the door opened and her friend appeared, looking a bit flustered.

"Oh! Hi Steph. I wasn't expecting you. Did you change your mind about closing the store early?"

"No. Paula, can I come in? I need to talk to you. It's important."

"Well..." Paula glanced over her shoulder. "Okay." As she stepped back from the door, Stephanie noticed that her friend's shirt was untucked and the buttons were fastened askew.

"I came at a bad time, didn't I?" She winced.

"Sort of, but that's okay. What's the matter? You look all worked up. And why do you have Coco with you?"

As they walked into the living room, a man rose from the sofa. After the brightness of the outdoors, Stephanie had a hard time seeing him. She assumed he was Paula's latest boyfriend. What was his name again? Jim? John? Jack? She couldn't recall, but smiled faintly at him. "Hi! Sorry to interrupt."

"No problem." He gave Stephanie a hard stare before walking towards the door. "Paula, I'm going to the store to get some beer. Want anything?"

Both women shook their heads and he grunted then left. Stephanie frowned as she finally got a good look at the man.

For some reason, she took an immediate dislike to Paula's latest beau. He seemed familiar—a bit like Jake with a similar build and colouring. Maybe that was it.

"So Steph, I don't mean to rush you, but Jack and I had plans, if you know what I mean, and I have to pick Chelsea up at the sitter's by five, so I'm on a bit of a tight schedule. What can I do for you?"

"Was that Jack, your new boyfriend?" Stephanie nodded towards the door the man had just exited through.

"Yeah, Jack Simms." Paula nodded and smiled. "Good looking isn't he? And really romantic, too. Did you know that one of the orders we made up today was for me? Wasn't that sweet?"

"Yeah—really sweet." She gave her head a shake. Paula's boyfriend wasn't important right now. "Listen, can you keep Coco for a while?"

"Sure, but I thought you said Jake liked cats."

"Maybe he does, I don't know. I don't know anything about him anymore." She stepped closer to her friend, checked over her shoulder to ensure that Jack had really left, then shared her awful discovery. "Paula, Jake's the stalker!"

"What?" Paula's eyes widened. "You're crazy. How can that be?"

"After we closed up, I went back to Jake's and decided to check the answering machine. You know how I always mess it up. Anyway, there was a message in this raspy voice, saying he was coming for me and the blood would be real this time." She shivered at the memory, but forced herself to continue. "I was scared and wanted to call Jake, but I didn't have his number, so I went looking through some drawers for a business card or something, instead I found a file with my name on it." She gripped her friend's arm. "Paula, it was full of pictures of me! At the mall, walking down a street. And there were copies of my birth certificate, my high school diploma. Why would Jake have all that stuff, if he wasn't stalking me?"

Paula's face had paled. "Geez, I can't think of a good reason. You must be right but what are you going to do?"

"Hide until the police find him."

"You can stay here." Paula moved as if to start looking for the most defensible position.

Steph stopped her. "Thanks, but it's too dangerous for you and Chelsea. If you could just keep Coco for me, it would be one less thing I have to worry about. Oh, and can you take care of the store? Hopefully, the police will catch him and I'll be back tomorrow, but just in case."

"Sure, I'll do anything I can." Paula worried her lip. "Where are you going?"

"I don't know. Maybe Ella's. I'm not sure if he'd know where she lives or not. Possibly into St. George and I'll take a room at a motel." She shook her head. "I can't think right now. All I know is that I have to get away."

Chapter 18

He sat crouched down, hidden in the back of her car, waiting for her to come out. His gun was poised in his hand ready to convince her to do as he said. It was amazing how easy this had turned out to be. He'd thought his plans for the day's activities had been ruined, but this was better than his original scheme. Stephanie would be seen driving out of town on her own. There was no way they'd be able to connect him to this.

The car door opened and he heard her getting in. "Bye Paula, I'll call you as soon as I'm settled tonight." Keys rattled on a chain and the engine started. He heard the gearshift move and felt the car going backward out of the driveway, curving to the left and onto the road, but then it paused. She shifted into park. Tensing, he wondered why she didn't immediately start driving away. Listening intently, he realized she was fumbling under the seat for something.

"Damn," she said. "Where's that cell phone? Maybe it slid into the back."

Hell! He quietly cocked the gun. Her seatbelt was being undone. The seat squeaked as she turned to look back. He raised his head, pointed the gun. "Hello Stephanie. Surprised to see me?"

The shocked look on her face was very satisfying. Her eyes widened. She opened her mouth and inhaled deeply, preparing to scream.

"Uh-uh-uh. Screaming wouldn't be a good idea right now. Just turn around and start to drive. Oh, and put your seatbelt back on. We wouldn't want to get a ticket now, would we?" She followed his commands and as she put the car into drive, he sat up. Crouching in the back was not only uncomfortable, but too difficult to keep the gun trained on her.

As he settled back in the seat, she beeped the horn twice. "What the hell did you do that for? " He leaned forward and pressed the gun to her temple.

Her eyes looked at his in the rear-view mirror and her voice trembled slightly. "I always beep twice when I leave Paula's. It's how we say goodbye. If I didn't, she'd think something was wrong."

He glanced back at Paula's house and thought he saw the front curtain move. Damn—had she seen that there was another occupant in the car? Possibly not, but just in case, once Stephanie was dealt with, Paula would have a little surprise of her own.

"Why are you doing this? What did I ever do to you?"

"You mean you haven't figured it out yet? I thought you were supposed to be a clever girl. We're old friends, Stephanie—I'm Jarrod Simpson." The car swerved as she reacted to the news. "Watch how you drive, bitch! I've already survived one car crash; I don't want to be in another."

"Sorry. I…I was just so surprised. You don't look the same as I remember." Her voice quivered and he smiled. He loved it when women were afraid.

"You know that car crash I just mentioned? It gave me this face. Reconstructive surgery can do wonders. I was such a mess that the doctors almost had a blank slate to start with, and the best part was that it was the other driver's fault. His insurance paid for everything." He laughed at the irony of it. "Once I had a new face, I got someone to make me a new identity and here I am today. Starting a new life by tying up some loose ends from my old life. And you, my dear Stephanie, are definitely one of those ends."

"But that was almost ten years ago."

"So? I'm like an elephant; I've got a good memory." The car stopped at a traffic light. "Turn left here."

"Why? Where are we going?"

"To see Ella. She's the other loose end."

"Ella!" Stephanie looked back at him. "She's just an old lady now. You don't want to hurt her."

"Why not? She screwed up my life. Because of you two, I did my first stint in jail. That deserves some payback."

"But it wasn't our fault. You started it!"

"Shut up. It *was* your fault." The memory of that night stirred the rage inside him. "You were just a scrawny little bitch. I paid attention to you and how did you pay me back? By accusing me of assault and attempted rape."

"Paid attention? Jarrod, you stole my money! You were mean and rude; always watching me and making suggestive comments. Then, that night, you hit me—"

"No! It wasn't like that! You thought you were too good for me, with your nose always stuck in a book. You wouldn't even stay in the same room as me. It was your fault! Now, just shut up! Shut up and drive." His breathing quickened as his memory of the events played out in his mind. She was just a stupid bitch. What did she know? He'd been paying attention to her and she'd ignored him. She deserved everything she got. Women were all the same. They didn't know their place, always complaining.

Just like his old lady had before his dad had shown her, taught her how to keep quiet. He could hear the old man's voice now. It played over and over in his head, while the sound of his mother's sobbing droned in the background. *"You can't be too nice 'cause they only understand one thing. Women are good for cooking and screwing, but only if you keep them in line. You remember that boy."*

Yeah, the old man was right, and now he'd make sure that Stephanie understood. She'd listen to him now or he'd teach her a lesson she'd never forget.

He wiped the sweat off his upper lip. The car was hot. He hated the heat. "Doesn't this damn car have air conditioning?"

"Yes." Her voice quavered. He liked that.

"Then turn it on." He watched as she fumbled with the controls, grunting in satisfaction as the air began to blow on him. "Glad this works. Better than the one at your house, right?"

"What?"

"The air conditioner at your house is broken; I did that. I did lots of things lately." He relaxed as the temperature in the car cooled. Leaning back in the seat, he gloated as he listed his accomplishments. "The thefts in town were all me, but the stupid cops couldn't figure it out. Your tires, your flowerbeds. I even siphoned the gas from your car one day. It was fun watching you fuss and fume when everything kept going wrong. You act like you're so calm and in control, but I had you jumping didn't I? Looking over your shoulder all the time." He chuckled at the memory. It had been fun teasing her, but this was better because now she knew it was him.

His fingers moved restlessly on the handle of the gun. He'd waited so long for this moment; he could hardly believe it was finally happening.

He sat up straighter and anxiously watched the street signs. They were almost there. Now, he'd make them sorry for what they had done. Stephanie would beg him for mercy and maybe, if she was good, he wouldn't kill her right away.

~~~

Stephanie pulled the car up to the curb in front of Ella McCreedy's house, the sight of it flooding her with happy memories. The place was old and large, a little in need of repair, but it still appeared warm and welcoming with its wide front porch and pots of geraniums on each step. Over the years, it had housed countless children; music and laughter spilling from windows and doors. Those days were gone now, Ella having been forced to give up fostering due to her bad knees and advancing age, but there was often a car in the driveway as past foster children, now adults, stopped by to visit.

Unfortunately, today wasn't one of those days.

The driveway was empty and so was the street. It was an older residential neighbourhood, occupied mostly by seniors now who were probably all inside, hiding from the intense summer heat.

Wiping her sweaty palms on the legs of her pants, Stephanie glanced back at her captor. He was staring at the house, muttering under his breath. Slowly her hand crept towards the door handle.

"Don't even think about it, Stephanie. I'll get out first and then it will be your turn." He opened the door and backed out, staying bent over, the gun still trained on her. "Now you get
~~~

out." She followed his command, keeping her eyes focused on the gun. "Good. Now walk up to the house. I'll be right behind you."

The gun pressed into her back as they walked up the steps, the cheery pots of pink geraniums starkly contrasting with the events that were unfolding. She hesitated before ringing the bell, but the prodding of the gun barrel had her lifting her hand and pressing the button. Hobbling steps could be heard crossing the floor and then the door swung open. Ella McCreedy looked out through the screen door and a smile spread across the older woman's face.

"Stephanie! What a surprise! First a phone call and now a visit." The screen door opened and she ushered her visitor in. A look of confusion crossed her face as Jarrod pushed his way in as well. "But, who is this?"

"I'm crushed that you don't recognize me, Ella. Don't you remember the foster kid you threw in jail? I'm Jarrod Simpson."

Stephanie stumbled farther into the house as Jarrod pushed her towards Ella. She caught herself and went to stand beside the older woman, putting a protective arm around her shoulders. Together they faced the man who was pointing a gun at them.

"Jarrod?"

"That's right, Ella. You told me that I wasn't to darken your door again, but I never was good at following orders, was I?" He waved his gun at them. "If I recall correctly, the living room is that way. We'll sit and talk in there."

Ella shuffled along, leaning heavily on her cane while Stephanie hovered beside her, casting anxious looks at the gun trained on them. They passed down the short hallway with its fading paper and scarred wainscoting, the wooden floors creaking slightly under their weight. The living room they entered was large and filled with mismatched furniture and bright coloured throw pillows all of which showed signs of wear. Ella's house had never been fancy but it had been warm and clean and most importantly filled with love.

Stephanie helped Ella to the sofa on the far side of the room. The older woman's knee was still swollen from the after effects of her surgery and she sat down with difficulty.

"Do you need a cushion or a stool for your leg, Ella?' Stephanie asked.

"Never mind! Her leg is the least of her worries right now." Jarrod's eyes were darting around the room. It hadn't changed much in the past ten years, and Stephanie wondered how much he remembered from his brief stay at the home.

Ella leaned back and settled her hands in her lap. "So Jarrod, what do you want? Are you hoping I'll cry and beg for mercy, or ask why you're doing this, just so you can spout off some long-winded speech about how life has done you wrong?" She shook her head. "Because if that's what you're hoping for, you're not going to get it from me. I don't scare easy and that gun doesn't impress me."

Stephanie gaped at Ella. Had the woman gone mad? Jarrod had a gun trained on them. Why was she taunting him? Stephanie turned to look at Jarrod. From the look on his face, he wasn't amused either. She scrambled to think of something to defuse the situation, when she saw a shadow moving in the hallway behind Jarrod. Someone else was in the house too.

Chapter 19

Jake had made his way carefully down the hallway, mindful of the creaking floorboards. Now he stood in the shadowed hallway, watching Ella put on her show. She was a feisty old girl and he admired her guts, but hoped it didn't get her killed. When he'd first arrived here, he'd had to undergo quite an interrogation about his intentions towards Stephanie. Ella might not be her mother, but she was certainly protective of her foster child.

Once Ella was sure he was a suitable companion, he'd explained why he was there. Of course, he'd glossed over the file of pictures saying Stephanie had been scared because of the message on the machine. Due to an argument they'd had that morning, she ran to hide rather than going to him. He wasn't sure if the woman had totally bought his explanation, but at least she hadn't thrown him out on his ear.

When he'd left the apartment, he'd debated about going to Paula's first, and had opted for Ella's house instead, deciding that Stephanie wouldn't want to put her friend's young daughter at risk. He'd thought he would wait at Ella's for a while, and, if Stephanie didn't show, he'd work his way back towards Paula's, possibly intercepting her along the way. Exactly what he'd been going to do when he found her, he hadn't quite decided. She thought he was the stalker, and he wasn't sure how to convince her otherwise; the evidence was pretty damning. However, he'd decided to cross that bridge when he got to it. Even if she was spitting fire at him or scared to death, as long as she was with him, he'd be able to protect her.

Well, she was here now, and he wouldn't have to explain that he wasn't the stalker since the man was in the living room right now, with a gun trained on both her and Ella. Ella knew he was here. He'd actually been in the bathroom when the doorbell had rung and had purposely lingered, wanting to give Stephanie some time to calm down before putting in an appearance. That, it turned out, had unwittingly been a stroke of genius. Now he'd have a chance to catch the other man off guard.

Jarrod Simpson had certainly thrown a wrench into things with his reappearance in Stephanie's life. All Jake's careful planning of a romantic courtship had been thrown out the window, and events had unfolded totally out of his control. He'd been so busy trying to keep pace with Stephanie, and resisting the call of the Elders, that his interpretation of Jarrod's intentions had been way off the mark. Now Stephanie was in danger and he had to try to find a way to save both her and Ella without revealing too much.

Standing just outside the doorway, he observed the man they were calling Jarrod pace across the room. The fellow was sweating heavily and kept wiping his hands on the leg of his pants, shifting the gun from one hand to the other. Jake wasn't one to watch crime shows, but even he could figure out that the fellow was nervous as hell, and dangerously unpredictable. Whatever plan of action Jake took, he'd have to be ready to deal with the fallout.

Once again, he focused on the action in the room. Ella had finished her spiel and Stephanie was looking shocked at the woman's boldness. Jarrod was seething.

"Shut up, you old cow. I should just blow a hole in your head right now. Is that what you want?" He levelled the gun at her. "Do you want to die first so you don't have to see what I do to your precious little girl? Well too bad. You can sit there and watch, and beg me not to hurt her." He turned the gun towards Stephanie. "Stand up and come here."

Stephanie slowly stood and walked towards Jarrod. Her face was white, and from his vantage point Jake could see the faint tremor of her chin. It was all he could do to not rush into the room. He clenched his fists and forced himself to wait.

Jarrod issued his next command. "Now, get down on your knees." She hesitated and he grabbed her hair, twisting and pulling downward.

She whimpered, pressing her lips tightly together and lowered herself to her knees.

Rage built inside Jake. He shook trying to maintain control.

Jarrod stroked the barrel of the gun across Stephanie's cheek. "Good girl. Now beg. Beg me to not hurt you. I want to hear you say my name and beg me to be nice."

When she didn't immediately comply, he slapped her across the face and she cried out, falling to the side. Ella shouted in outrage and lunged forward, striking out at him with her cane. Jarrod stumbled as the wooden stick made contact with his knee.

Knowing this might be his best opportunity, Jake rushed into the room, knocking Jarrod the rest of the way off his feet. The gun went off and bits of plaster dust rained down on them from the ceiling. The two men struggled, then Jake managed to grab the other man's wrist, applying pressure until the gun dropped from Jarrod's hand. It skittered across the floor coming to a rest a few feet away. Shoving Jarrod away, Jake quickly turned to pick up the weapon, only to gasp as he felt a searing pain slice through his arm. The other man had had a knife concealed on him and was now wielding it.

After that, everything seemed to happen in slow motion. Not pausing, despite the blood that was dripping down his arm, Jake grabbed the gun, curling his fingers around the cool metal, pivoting and swinging the weapon upwards towards his assailant all in one smooth flowing motion. In the background, he could hear Steph and Ella, but didn't have time to register what they were saying. What seemed like ages actually only took a split second to occur and Jake suddenly found himself face to face with Jarrod. The other man's arm was raised, ready to strike a deadly blow to his chest.

They froze, facing each other, both with deadly intent.

Jake stared up at his opponent and curled his lip. "A bullet is faster than a knife."

Jarrod hesitated, his arm indecisively hovering in mid-air before he lowered his weapon in defeat and stepping back.

Behind him, Jake could hear the ladies breathe a sigh of relief. He straightened, keeping the gun fixed on his opponent as he barked out orders. "Drop the knife. Now keep backing up, right over there to that chair."

The other man sullenly retreated and sat down, his eyes full of rage.

Jake took a deep breath and let it out in a whoosh. That had been close. Keeping one eye on his prisoner, he stepped towards Stephanie and Ella intent on seeing how they were doing, only to stiffen when he heard a sound behind him.

"Get away from them, Jake!"

Turning, he saw Paula, standing in the doorway with a gun trained on him. "Paula!"

"I said, get away from them. I know how to use this gun, don't make me show you!" Paula was pale, but her face was grim and determined, her arms braced. She swallowed hard and adjusted her grip on the gun.

Everyone began speaking simultaneously.

"Paula, I can explain—" Jake began, lowering his weapon as a precaution.

"Paula, you've got it all wrong—" Stephanie cried out from her crouched position on the floor.

"Paula, sweetheart..." Jarrod rose from the chair he'd been sitting in, extending his hand towards her.

Paula's eyes swung from Jake, to Stephanie and then to Jarrod, her confusion evident. She half lowered the gun and stepped towards the man she viewed as her boyfriend. "Jack? What are you doing here?"

"No!" The other occupants of the room called out in unison, but it was too late. Jarrod had pulled the gun from Paula's hand. He spun her around, pinning her to him and pressed the gun against her throat. Everyone froze.

"Jack! What are you doing?" Paula's eyes looked like large black pools of fear in her pale face.

"Shut up, Paula! And my name is Jarrod not Jack."

"Jarrod? But, but..." Paula stammered.

"Yeah, Jarrod. Jarrod Simpson. Didn't Stephanie ever tell you about me?"

"Well, yes, but—"

"Good. Now shut up and let me think."

Rising from the floor, Stephanie spoke in a trembling voice. "Jarrod, let her go. It's me you want."

Jake took a half step forward, his heart pounding in fear. "No!"

"Don't move! None of you move, or I'll kill her." Jarrod's eyes darted over their faces while his grip on Paula tightened. A small whimper came from her, tears rolling down her face as the gun pressed harder against her throat.

The room was silent except for the ticking of the clock as everyone stared at the gun-wielding man, wondering what his next move might be. Jake tried to keep his face impassive as he assessed the situation, calculating the odds of being able to successfully carry out a frontal assault. As much as he wanted to step forward and wrench the gun from Jarrod's hand, he had to consider the safety of the other occupants of the room. If it was only himself that he had to worry about, he wouldn't care, but there were three women to consider and who knew where a stray bullet might end up? While he was confident that he could help one injured person, multiple casualties in rapid succession might be too taxing on his abilities. No. He'd have to wait for the right opportunity.

Jarrod finally spoke. "All right. This is what's going to happen. Everyone head upstairs. Stephanie you lead the way to your old bedroom. I know the door will be solid, since Ella must've replaced the one I broke. I'll lock you all in there while I make some phone calls, then we're going to go for a little ride together."

Jarrod waved his gun and ushered them towards the stairs. Jake helped Ella up and they slowly made their way up the stairs to the second floor.

Chapter 20

As the door slammed shut behind them, Stephanie found her arms full of a sobbing Paula. Over her friend's shoulder, she saw Jake watching her. She gave him a look that she hoped said 'we'll talk in a minute' before she concentrated on trying to make sense of Paula's rambling confession.

"I'm sorry, I'm sorry. I thought Jake had his gun pointed at you, Stephanie. You told me he was the stalker and when I heard you beep the horn when you left my house, I remembered how much you hated it when people did that, so I looked out the window and I thought I saw Jake in the car holding a gun. I came over here to rescue you." She finally paused for a breath and Stephanie was able to get a word in.

"It's all right Paula. I thought Jake was the stalker too, but he wasn't. It's Jarrod, or Jack—whatever you want to call him." She took her friend's face in her hands and wiped the tears from her cheeks. "You did fine, Paula. You picked up on my hint that something was wrong, called the police and tried to rescue me." Stephanie paused as she noted a guilty look washing over her friend's face. "Paula, you did call the police, didn't you?"

Paula bit her lip and looked down at the floor. "Well, I was so worried about you, I just grabbed my keys and jumped in the car, completely forgetting to call them before I left the house. Then, I was going to use my cell phone and call as I drove over here, but you know how I never charge the battery until it's dead."

Stephanie held back the frustrated scream that was growing inside her and instead gave her friend a quick hug. Paula always had good intentions, but seldom thought things through as thoroughly as she should.

"That's okay. Don't worry. We'll think of something." Paula looked rather pale and Stephanie felt sorry for her. Not only had her friend forgotten to call the police, but she'd managed to get them all captured and then, to top things off, her new boyfriend was a criminal. If the situation hadn't been so grave, she could have laughed. Once again, Paula's love life was running true to form.

Looking around, Stephanie noticed that Jake had helped Ella to lie down on the bed and was rubbing the older woman's leg. Leaving Paula, Steph hurried over and took her foster mother's hand. "Ella, are you all right?"

"Yes, Sweetie, I'm fine. I twisted my knee when I swung that cane at Jarrod. It's strange though. It hurt real bad downstairs, but now that Jake has me all propped up and comfy here, it feels just fine. If I didn't know better, I'd almost think I'd never had surgery."

Stephanie cast an inquiring look at Jake. He met her gaze for a moment and then looked away, but not before she'd seen the flash of concern in his eyes.

"Perhaps it just popped back into place," he suggested. He walked over to the door and turned the handle experimentally, then began checking the hinges.

"Could be." Ella watched him thoughtfully for a moment before glancing at Stephanie. "I hate to say it, but Jarrod was right. This house is old and most of the rooms have really poor fitting doors, but this one is new and tight as a drum."

"What about the windows?" Having given up on the door, Jake started to examine them.

"Old as the hills and painted shut, last time I checked." Ella shook her head. "Since I stopped fostering a while back, I haven't had to keep these rooms up."

"We could break them," Stephanie suggested. "But it's a long way down."

"And Jack, er, Jarrod would hear the breaking glass and be up the stairs before even one of us got out." Paula added pessimistically, plopping down in the lone chair and pulling her knees up to her chin. She began to nervously chew on her thumbnail.

"So..." Stephanie stared around the room. "We'll have to think of something else." By now Jake was sitting on the floor, his head resting against the wall, apparently deep in thought. She wondered what he was thinking. Did he know that she'd thought he was the stalker? He must have gone to the apartment, found the pictures scattered all over and decided to go looking for her, though how he'd known to come to Ella's, she wasn't sure. Hesitantly, she sat down beside him, hoping he wasn't too angry with her.

Silently, she chastised herself. She was supposed to be the calm, logical one and what had she done? Jumped to conclusions and, as a result, landed them all in this mess. Officer Carter had placed a few seeds of doubt in her mind; the taped message and the pictures had just seemed to confirm everything.

The room was quiet, each lost in their own thoughts. Stephanie went over recent events and wondered how her peaceful, orderly life could have turned so upside down in just a week. Glancing over at Paula, she recalled how her friend had proclaimed that a new haircut would be the start of a whole new life. Somehow, this wasn't quite what she had envisioned.

"I'm sorry." She spoke in a low voice, not wanting the others to hear her confession.

"For what?" He turned his head to look at her.

"For doubting you." She flicked a glance at him and then looked away, ashamed of herself. How could she have thought such a vile thing about him when all he'd ever done was be kind and patient and supportive? "I thought you were the stalker."

"It's okay." One corner of his mouth quirked upward. "The evidence was pretty damning."

She nodded. Now was not the time to ask why he had a file of pictures of her.

Jake shifted beside her and she looked at him, her eyes taking in the strained lines around his mouth, his clenched fists, the blood on his wrist. She gasped. In all of the confusion, she'd forgotten that Jarrod had cut him with the knife. "Jake!"

He shushed her, nodding toward the other side of the room. Ella's eyes were closed as were Paula's. Whether they were resting or thinking, she wasn't sure, but she lowered her voice. "Jake, your arm! Let me see." She grabbed his arm, frantically looking for the wound. "Where's the cut? I know you're hurt. There's dried blood on your arm."

"Stephanie, don't fuss. I'm fine." He whispered the words to her, his eyes darting towards Paula and Ella.

"But Jake, it doesn't make sense. There should be a cut somewhere." She twisted his arm this way and that, once again trying to locate the source of the blood, then began pulling at the body of his shirt, thinking the wound was somewhere else.

"Steph." He managed to catch her hands in his and she stopped her search. "I'm fine. I... I heal quickly."

"Jake, no one heals that fast."

"I do." He stared directly into her eyes. It was almost as if he were trying to tell her something, hoping she'd see something or recognize something.

"I don't understand."

"Steph, it's hard to explain right now. It's like a...a gift that I have. I can heal myself. Others, too." He reached out and stroked her face. The vague throbbing of her cheek from Jarrod's slap immediately faded away.

Stephanie reached up and touched her face in wonder. "It doesn't hurt anymore."

"I'm glad." He continued to cradle her face, a soft smile playing over his lips as he took in her features.

"Jake, how did you do that? How is that possible?"

"Stephanie, I'll try to explain it all to you later, but it's important right now that no one else knows this. Not Ella, not Paula, not anyone. It has to be our secret, please?"

She frowned but nodded.

"Listen, I will get you out of this. I haven't waited this long just to lose you again."

"Again?"

"Yes. Again. There isn't time to explain it properly right now, but just remember that I love you. I've always loved you and I'll never—"

The bedroom door swung open, and Jarrod stepped into the room. "Okay, everything is ready. I've got a friend downstairs with a van. He'll do the driving while I keep an eye on you guys. First we'll head over to Paula's so I can get some stuff from my car and then we'll go for a nice, long drive. Come on, get up." He waved his gun at them.

Reluctantly, they got to their feet and moved downstairs. Instinctively, Stephanie started to turn towards the front door, which was the entrance that was always used. Jarrod put out his arm, blocking her.

"We're not going out that way. We'll use the back door. There's less chance of being seen."

Stephanie tightened her hands into fists. Being seen by one of the neighbours had been her only hope. The backyards were small and led to a seldom-used alleyway. The likelihood of attracting attention from there was slim.

Jarrod herded them into the kitchen and towards the back door. Just before opening it, he issued a warning. "Be quiet and don't do anything stupid. I have this gun and my friend in the van has one, too."

The four captives exchanged worried glances before stepping outside.

The house sported an old covered porch with a wooden railing around the edges. In its day, it had been quite grand, but now the paint was peeling and the boards creaked under their feet. It was also high up, due to the sloping nature of the backyard. Steep steps led from the wooden platform down to the ground level. Stephanie still remembered when the new steps had been installed. Ella had always intended to have a handrail added on to them, but it had never materialized. As a result, the exit was seldom used anymore.

As they crossed the porch, Ella hesitated near the top of the stairs, quite probably unsure of being able to navigate them with her knee.

"Ella, let Paula and I get on each side of you. You can hang on to us to keep yourself steady." Stephanie suggested, moving to stand beside the older woman.

"Hurry up, quit stalling!" Impatiently, Jarrod shoved the older woman and she stumbled. Paula reached out to steady her while Stephanie turned to chastise him.

"Leave her alone! She's just had knee surgery."

"I said be quiet!" Jarrod backhanded her across the face, the barrel of the gun hitting her forehead. Blood spurted from the cut.

With a growl of rage, Jake grabbed Jarrod by the front of his shirt, swinging him around and nearly lifting the man off his feet. Jarrod jerked backwards, causing a chain reaction as everyone bumped into each other, exclaiming loudly as they scrambled to keep from falling down the steep stairs. Momentarily distracted, Jake glanced over to see what was happening. His small lapse in concentration was all the opening that Jarrod needed.

"I've had enough of you." And without further notice, Jarrod shot him.

The sound echoed between the buildings as did Stephanie's scream. In horror, she watched Jake's eyes widen as he stumbled backwards crashing into the porch railing. The old wood broke under the force of his weight and he fell to the ground below, a red stain rapidly spreading across the front of his shirt.

"Jake!" Heedless of those around her, Stephanie scrambled down the steps and ran to his side. She pressed her hand to his chest, trying to stem the bleeding but it oozed between her fingers. "Jake? Can you hear me? Oh God." She leaned over him and his eyes fluttered open.

"Steph?" He tried to reach up to her.

"I'm here, Jake." She caught his hand and held it to her face, pressing a kiss against his palm. His fingers trembled against her cheek, sliding up towards her hair, touching the cut on her forehead.

"Steph, I lo—" Suddenly, his hand fell limp in hers and his eyes went blank, his face lax.

"No! No! Jake! Jake!" She knew she was screaming but she couldn't stop. There was a roaring sound in her ears. Hands were pulling at her. Dragging her backwards. She fought against the arms that wrapped around her waist and shoved her into the back of the waiting van. Even as the door slammed shut she flung herself against it, pressing her blood-covered hands against the rear window. As the van sped away down the alley, kicking up clouds of dust, her last glimpse of Jake was of his lifeless body lying abandoned on the blood-stained ground.

~~~

Jake could sense the blood pouring from his body with each pump of his heart. Strange how the very organ that had kept him alive all these years was now helping his life's blood seep away. He was cold. So very cold. But at least the pain was fading and the heaviness was being replaced with a sense of lightness as he floated above himself. He could see the red stain spreading on the ground, his own eyes staring blankly up at the sky. It had been a good life...

The tingling energy of the universe began to absorb his spirit. A sense of oneness, of homecoming was filling him. Looking down he saw his lifeless body sprawled on the grass. He gazed around at the trees and the flowerbeds nearby, wondering if he would miss seeing them; he'd always been partial to nature. A loud sound drew his attention and, as his vision began to fade, he noted a van careening down the alley, knocking over garbage cans as it raced away, a blood-covered hand pressed against the rear window.
~~~

Chapter 21

Jarrod sat in the back of the van guarding the three women. They were silent, except for the occasional sob that came from Stephanie. Paula was holding her while Ella sat ramrod straight staring defiantly at him. He glared at her, but then glanced away.

There was something about the old biddy that always made him feel uncomfortable, like she could see right inside him. He wondered if she knew how much he hated her; how his stomach was clenching right now and that he was sweating bullets trying to figure a way out of this mess.

He'd bluffed his way through the first part, telling his friend Murray, who was driving the van, that he'd hit pay dirt and was going to give him a big cut for his help. Murray thought the old lady was worth something and they were holding her for ransom. He wouldn't be happy when he found out she wasn't, but Jarrod decided to worry about that later.

His fingers twitched nervously on the gun he still held tightly in his hand. He'd have to get rid of it somewhere, but right now, he needed it to keep his prisoners in line. Damn, but everything was going wrong. He'd planned on breezing into town, making a little money and settling his score with Stephanie before heading on his way.

Now he'd killed that guy and the body was out in plain sight. There were three witnesses, too. Four, if he counted Murray. He'd have to do something about them. A shudder ran through him. He hated it when things got messy like this. Thinking on his feet wasn't his strong point, but now he'd have to. There were all these women to kill, and maybe Murray, too, if the man proved to be skittish.

The van turned a corner sharply and they all had to brace themselves to keep from sliding.

"Slow down, Murray! You want us to get pulled over for speeding? And turn up the damned air conditioner, it's hot back here." Jarrod cuffed the sweat from his upper lip and glanced out the window. "Dammit Murray, you took the wrong exit! Now we're headed for the highway. Use the next off ramp and get this thing turned around!"

Murray muttered something back at him, but Jarrod decided to ignore it for now. He'd settle his score with the other man later. Soon they'd be back at Paula's house. His car was there, and he needed to make a few more phone calls. The loot he'd stolen had to be quickly liquidated. He'd take a hit on the price he'd get for it but that couldn't be helped. He needed some ready cash now if he was to put as much distance as possible between himself and Weston.

Thoughtfully, he considered the women. Originally, he'd only planned on taking Stephanie, but he hadn't been able to decide what to do with the others so he'd opted for bringing them all along. Now he realized that three people would be too much trouble. He'd have to get rid of them somehow. Maybe he could arrange some type of accident. A car crash? A gas explosion? A break-in gone bad?

Yeah, that would work. He could make it look like Paula and her friends came home and found a thief in her house. The robber shoots at them, Paula shoots and kills the guy but not before he shoots them. They all bleed to death... He eyed Murray speculatively and shrugged. They hadn't known each other long and he didn't want to have to pay the man anyway.

~~~

Stephanie sat frozen within Paula's arms, aware that others were around her, but too taken up with her own grief to really register what was going on. Jake was dead and she felt this awful emptiness inside her. He'd been killed trying to defend her, yet just hours before she'd been thinking such bad thoughts about him. She'd thought he was a stalker, but he wasn't. He was really a wonderful man who had just happened to come into her flower shop one day, and now she'd never see him again.

The van hit a bump and she was jostled in the seat, her head bouncing against the wall. She winced slightly and reached up
~~~

distractedly to rub the bump. Her hand encountered the stickiness of blood and she stared at it, wondering where it had come from. Oh, right, Jarrod had hit her and cut her head. Feeling around she frowned. There was no tender spot, no pain.

Hmm... Jake had said he could heal people. Had his last act been to heal the cut on her head? She recalled his fingers moving over her face and felt fresh tears welling up in her eyes. He should have been trying to heal himself rather than worrying about her. 'Oh, Jake!' She thought, picturing him lying on the ground.

'Stephanie.' A voice whispered in her ear. It sounded just like him.

She jerked and sat up straight, looking around the van in surprise. No one else seemed to have heard it. Ella was glaring at Jarrod. Jarrod was looking at the driver, and Paula had her eyes closed, her lips moving, perhaps in silent prayer.

Stephanie blinked several times. Okay, she was upset. Perhaps she just thought she'd heard Jake's voice. Jake was...dead. Swallowing hard at the unpalatable thought, she tried to make her body relax.

'Steph? Are you there?'

"What?" She spoke out loud and everyone looked at her. Paula squeezed her hand and Jarrod stared at her, a muscle twitching in his jaw. Ella gave her an encouraging nod. Stephanie smiled wanly at her friends and then turned to stare blankly out the window, her mind racing.

It was Jake's voice, she was sure of it, but Jake was gone. It couldn't be. Could it?

'Steph, don't say anything. Just know that I'm here with you. I'll never leave you. Everything will be fine once you get to Paula's. Just stay in the van.'

A feeling of warmth filled her, chasing away the darkness that had consumed her just moments before. She sat up straighter, confused but positive she wasn't imagining things. In some inexplicable way, Jake was here, and she felt comforted by the fact that his spirit was with her.

Stephanie began to take in her surroundings with a critical eye. They were almost at Paula's. She didn't know what fate awaited them, but she was ready to respond in whatever way was needed. She reached over and squeezed Paula's hand. The two friends stared at each other and Stephanie nodded imperceptibly. Paula nodded back. Ever since they'd met, there had been a bond between them, an understanding of the other that went beyond words. Neither knew what was going on, but they were both ready to act as a team, if needed.

The van pulled up in front of Paula's. Jarrod grunted instructions at the driver. "I'm going to the car to get my stuff. You take the women inside the house." The two men climbed out. Jarrod walked towards his vehicle and Murray circled around to the back.

Knowing she had but a moment, Stephanie quickly whispered instructions. "Don't leave the van."

"Why?" Paula asked.

"I'm not sure. Something is just telling me that we should stay in here."

"All right." The other two hesitantly agreed, exchanging puzzled glances.

Murray was pulling the rear door open when suddenly Jarrod could be heard shouting and the sounds of a scuffle filled the air. Murray turned, leaving the door partially ajar. Stephanie promptly forgot she'd been told to stay in the van and quietly crept forward. In passing, she wondered what was happening to her usually timid self. A week ago, she would have been cowering in the corner.

Through the crack in the door, she could see Murray pulling out his gun. Biting her lip, she wondered what to do. She wasn't sure what was happening outside, but if she managed to incapacitate Murray, it could only improve their chances. Suddenly, Paula was beside her. They exchanged glances and, in unspoken agreement, grabbed the rear door and swung it out as hard as they could. It hit Murray in the back with a satisfying thud, sending the man sprawling onto his face.

"We did it!" They congratulated each other with high fives and, after gesturing for Paula to wait, Stephanie cautiously stepped out of the van. Peering around the edge of the door, she tried to see where Jarrod was. Spotting his body lying on the ground near his car, she moved away from the relative protection of the door only to feel a pair of strong hands grab her and spin her around. She screamed in fear, not sure who it might be.

"Steph?" A deep voice spoke her name. She looked up and gasped. It was…

"Jake!" She launched herself into his arms, raining kisses on his face while running her hands over him, hardly daring to believe that he was actually there. "Oh Jake, I can't believe it's you. I was sure you were dead." Tears of joy were streaming down her face as she looked up at him.

He cradled her face, looking deeply into her eyes, his own full of light, joy and...? Before she could decide on a name for the emotion, he pulled her to him, kissing her thoroughly, his mouth devouring hers while his hands roamed through her hair then over her body before pressing her tightly against him. Lost in the wonder of the kiss, she ground herself against him. She'd thought she would never again feel him, taste him, see him. Pulling away, she smiled up at him, his name coming out on a heartfelt sigh. "Oh Jake."

Suddenly he was pushing her away, his hands gripping her shoulders and giving her a little shake. "What the hell did you think you were doing? I told you to wait in the van, not play superwoman and try to catch the bad guys."

"What?" Her pleasure at seeing him alive rapidly evaporated under his accusing stare. "What do you mean, what was I doing? I was trying to save myself and Paula and Ella."

"I told you, I'd take care of everything. What if I hadn't managed to knock out Jarrod? It could have been him grabbing you instead of me. You need to learn to listen—"

"Excuse me? I don't take orders from you!" Stephanie felt her temper rising. She seldom got mad, but when she did the heat of her ire matched the red highlights in her hair. "So what if Jarrod was still out there? At least we got rid of one bad guy and improved the odds."

"That's not the point. What if you'd been hurt? I might not be strong enough yet to help you! It was a foolish risk. You can't just go rushing headlong into dangerous situations—"

"Foolish! How dare you—"

"Umm, don't mind us." Paula tapped both of them on the shoulder and in unison their heads swivelled to look at her. She grinned at them impishly. "Before the fireworks start, Ella and I are just going into the house. We've tied up the bad guys with some duct tape we found in Jarrod's car. Once you're done, you can come inside and explain to us why Jake's not dead, and how the cut on Stephanie's face has healed." With that, the two women walked away.

Stephanie and Jake watched them disappear with equally stunned expressions, then looked from Jarrod's body to Murray's. Sure enough, they were trussed up like turkeys, duct tape neatly binding their arms and legs. Finally, they looked at each other, eyes narrowed, considering.

Jake ran his hand through his hair and sighed. Reaching out, he gently put his hand on Stephanie's shoulder. "I'm sorry Steph. I guess I'm still recovering from our recent scare and I'm a bit angry at myself too, but I shouldn't be taking it out on you. If I'd been home this afternoon instead of trying to hunt down Jarrod on my own, you wouldn't have been alone, found that file or gone running off."

His hand was warm and heavy on her shoulder, a comforting weight. She let it rest there a moment while he spoke, but then stepped back, suddenly unsure of how she felt. A million questions raced through her mind. Paula was right. Why wasn't he dead? And why did he have a complete file on her? In all the excitement, she'd forgotten about that.

She was just going to ask the first of many questions, when the screeching of tires drew her attention. Two police cars had come to rest in front of Paula's house, little bits of debris stirring in their wake. The officers quickly exited, took up protective positions behind the vehicles and drew their weapons, pointing them at Jake.

"Step away from the woman and no one will get hurt." One of the officers said in an authoritative voice.

Looking from the police to Jake and back again, Stephanie started to explain. "It's okay. There's been a mistake." She reached out to grab Jake's hand.

"Step away." The stern, uncompromising voice had Stephanie jerking her hand back. "Stay back, ma'am. You're safe now. We've got him covered."

Slowly Jake raised his hands and Stephanie stepped back, still sputtering in protest even though her words fell on deaf ears. The police cautiously approached Jake, guns trained on him. After being ordered to kneel and to put his hands on his head, he was cuffed and dragged to his feet.

As the police holstered their weapons, Stephanie grabbed one of the officers by the arm, pleading with him to listen. "What's going on? He hasn't done anything wrong. Look over there, those are the bad guys." The officer glanced towards where Jarrod and Murray lay. Other police were now dragging them to their feet and a general sense of confusion seemed to be filling the air. Ella and Paula had come back outside and were now standing on the porch, watching the proceedings with concern.

"Ma'am, we've had a report of an armed man, a possible hostage situation and a stalker all at this address. Apparently this man, Jacob St. Clair has been stalking a local woman and threatening her with bodily harm."

"But that's me! I'm the woman he's been stalking!" She shouted in frustration while gesturing wildly.

The officer raised his eyebrows and realizing how that had sounded, she tried to back-pedal.

"No. What I meant was that I'm the woman that was being stalked, but it wasn't this man who was doing it. I'm Stephanie Fields and the stalker is that man over there, Jarrod Simpson, except he's been going around calling himself Jack Simms."

The police officer looked from Jake to Jarrod and then back at Stephanie, obviously not sure what to make of things. Another police car pulled up and Stephanie didn't know whether to laugh or cry when she saw Officer Carter get out and walk over.

Frowning as he was briefed on the situation, Officer Carter scratched his head then began to question Stephanie. "Miss Fields, you left a rather frantic message for me this afternoon, claiming that Mr. St. Clair was the stalker. Do you care to explain that?"

Stephanie stared at Jake for a moment. He seemed to be holding his breath. After a brief pause, she responded. "Did I say Jake? I guess I was so upset that I didn't know what I was saying. I meant Jack, my friend Paula's new boyfriend. Jarrod Simpson has been in town for the past few months posing as Jack Simms. He struck up an acquaintance with my friend and assistant, Paula."

"And how did you determine that he was the stalker?"

"I, ah, recognized his voice on the answering machine."

"I see." The man gave her a doubtful look. "And how did you end up over here?"

Stephanie thought quickly and began to give a much edited version of the day's events. "Well, once I realized that it was Paula's boyfriend, I hurried over to her house to warn her. After talking to her I got back in my car and Jarrod, or Jack, was hiding in the back seat and forced me to go to Ella's, then Jake and Paula both arrived, but Jarrod had a gun and shot at Jake, then took us hostage and brought us back over here." She paused for breath hardly able to believe she'd been able to string a lie together that quickly.

Carter raised his eyebrows and Jake jumped in to continue the story.

"I was actually only nicked by the bullet and a bit stunned from falling off the porch. Once I got my wits about me, I got in Stephanie's car and came over here, remembering that Jarrod had said he needed to get some things from his vehicle. I found Stephanie's cell phone on the floor of her car and called the police to meet me over here. Then I waited in the bushes for Jarrod to arrive and managed to disarm him."

Stephanie added a few more details. "I was inside the van with Paula and Ella and saw that Murray—that's the fellow who was helping Jarrod—was distracted so we, Paula and I, knocked him out by hitting him in the back with the van door. Then Ella and Paula tied them up with duct tape so they couldn't escape."

"Hmm... I guess that makes sense." Officer Carter looked up from the notepad he'd been rapidly scribbling in.

"Of course it makes sense, young man!" Ella spoke from behind them and they all started. Stephanie wondered how long she'd been there and how much she'd heard. "Now let this poor man go and do what you're paid for. Gather up the bad guys and haul them off to jail!"

"Yes, ma'am." The younger officer jumped to do Ella's bidding. Officer Carter nodded and flipped his notebook shut. "I might have further questions for you later, but for now, you've all had a hard day so I suggest you head home."

Inwardly breathing a sigh of relief, Stephanie watched as they removed the cuffs from Jake's wrists. She held his hand tight as Jarrod and Murray were taken away. Jarrod kept looking over at Jake, his face white as a sheet, almost as if he thought he'd seen a ghost. Jake took half a step towards the man and then gave an amused grunt as Jarrod all but dived into the back of the cruiser.

Stephanie gave Ella a hug and they fussed over each other, offering words of reassurance and relief that this particular ghost from their past had been dealt with. Laughing at a comment Ella had made, Steph glanced at Jake and noted that he was standing very alert, his eyes sharply studying each of the remaining policemen. Finally his gaze rested on an officer that was walking over towards Paula. His eyes narrowed. Frowning, Stephanie wondered why Jake seemed so interested in the man. Did they know each other from somewhere?

Just then Ella grabbed Jake's arm and, with a start, he looked down at her, apparently losing his interest in the policeman. Ella poked him in the chest. "You sure looked dead back at my house and I've seen dead before."

"Umm, I just bleed easily." Jake smiled at her disarmingly, but Ella remained unmoved.

"Humph! Right. And I'm Grandma Moses." Ella grabbed his chin, turning his face this way and that.

"Ella! What are you doing?" Stephanie asked in a shocked tone. Ella was usually so affable.

"I'm just checking to see if his nose is growing from telling all those lies."

"It was all the truth. Mostly." Jake said sheepishly, shifting about a bit. Stephanie bit back a smile. Having been on the receiving end of Ella's brand of interrogation, she knew just how he felt.

"Uh-huh. Listen you two, I've been around a long time and I've seen some pretty strange things in my life. I don't know what's going on and I don't really care, just so long as you're safe and happy." She put her hands on her hips and gave them both a pointed stare. "Any time you want to explain all of this to me you can, otherwise I'll just sit at home and wait for an invitation to the wedding."

Jake cleared his throat. "Ella, there are some things it's best not to know, but when the proper time comes, I will tell you what I can."

"That's all I'm asking for, son. Now you two better go talk to Paula because I've got a feeling that you need to corroborate some stories. I'll be waiting in the car for a ride home."

They did indeed have to get their stories straight with Paula in case the police questioned her. Finding her busily batting her eyelashes at one of the policemen, Stephanie managed to get her away and into the house where the three of them could talk in private. After hearing them relate the story that Jake had told the police, Paula frowned.

"I could have sworn that bullet hit you in the chest! And there was blood everywhere."

"You were so upset it probably seemed like it was more serious than it was." Stephanie suggested, hoping her friend would buy the excuse.

"But, that doesn't even look like the same shirt you had on earlier." Paula looked puzzled, staring at the small blood stain near the side seam of Jake's shirt.

"Paula, does it really matter?" Stephanie asked in exasperation. She knew for a fact that Jake had indeed changed shirts somehow. Ella always had spare clothes at the house, so he'd probably found one there and had disposed of the original blood soaked one. And that small 'blood' stain looked suspiciously like ketchup.

"Umm, I'll just wait in the car." Jake beat a hasty retreat, obviously deciding he'd had enough of Paula's interrogation.

"Paula, you know how I came here and said I thought Jake was the stalker, but he really wasn't? Well, do you think that you could just forget about that part if the police ask you about it?"

With a nod, Paula agreed to use Stephanie's version of the events, still upset over her unwitting contribution to the whole fiasco. "I still can't believe what a rotten, lying bastard that Jack turned out to be! He was only nice to me to get to you!" Paula stood with her hands on her hips looking totally affronted for a moment before realizing that she was missing the big picture. "Oh! I'm sorry Steph. Not that what he did to you wasn't more rotten."

Stephanie laughed and hugged her friend. "It's all right, Paula. I know it's a shock to you that the man wasn't blown away by your beauty and charm."

Paula had opened her mouth to protest, but Stephanie leaped in with a laughing apology.

"I'm sorry. I'm just teasing you. For some reason, I'm almost feeling giddy right now. After effects from what happened, no doubt. Listen, Jake's in the car and we have some stuff we have to talk about. Do you think you'll be okay here, by yourself?"

"Me? The romance queen? I only knew the man a few days. We didn't even sleep together. I'll eat some ice cream, watch a sappy movie and be ready to move on tomorrow. You know that one policeman that was here? He's new in town. His name is Matt, he's gorgeous and he's got the sexiest Scottish accent. I offered to show him around, help him get settled. You know." Paula grinned and winked.

"Are you sure?" Stephanie often wondered if her friend was really as unaffected by her break-ups as she appeared to be. Paula had a big heart, but she hid it under a flippant facade. Their eyes met and Paula sobered for a moment.

"I'll be fine, really. You go and straighten things out with Jake. He's a good man and he's right for you. I know it." Paula gave her a hug and pushed her friend out the door. "Oh, and don't forget Coco!"

Stephanie looked around and saw the pet carrier with Coco still inside. The animal was glaring at her, its tail swishing from side to side. Someone was not a happy camper about having been cooped up for several hours.

As Stephanie walked towards the car, she wondered if what Paula said was true or not. Was Jake right for her? Yes, he'd helped to save her today, but there was something that he was hiding.

It was for Ella and Paula's sake that she was brushing off his injuries as minor, but she knew differently; she'd been right beside him when he was bleeding on the ground. There was no logical explanation for his recovery. And then there were all those pictures of her at his apartment. He hadn't just noticed her and decided to make her acquaintance. Jake had been stalking her, but why?

She eyed him as she approached the car. He was helping Ella into the back seat and looked harmless enough, but was he really who he said he was? Could she trust him? That remained to be seen.

Chapter 22

Paula had been sufficiently distracted by the fact that Jack Simms was Jarrod Simpson that she hadn't asked about why Jake had a file full of pictures of her friend. Jake was sure, however, that Stephanie had not forgotten and he was dreading the upcoming conversation. Everything hinged on his ability to convince Stephanie that his story was true. But, after all that had happened today, he wondered how receptive she would be. Mentally, he crossed his fingers and hoped that his faith in destiny was not misplaced.

After they left Paula's they'd taken Ella home. Surprisingly, she hadn't asked awkward questions, instead chatting about how tired she was from all the excitement. Stephanie helped her into the house and got her settled, promising to call the next day. Then she was back in the car and they were heading across town again to his place.

The drive was completed in silence except for Coco's pathetic wailing. Once inside the apartment, the cat ran off and hid under the armchair, her tail swishing back and forth in disapproval of the shabby treatment she'd been receiving.

Jake and Stephanie stood facing each other, an awkward silence growing between them as neither was sure where to begin. Finally Stephanie sighed, dropped down onto the couch, and leaned her head wearily against the cushions. She closed her eyes and rubbed her hands over her face. Jake wondered what she was thinking, but felt it best to let her begin. Finally, she opened her eyes, looked at him and began talking.

"So, you're telling me that you have this supernatural power to heal yourself and other people?"

"Sort of. I can heal cuts, burns, broken bones, things like that, but not diseases or stop the aging process. That's part of a person's genetics and I have no control over that." He stood before her, his hands in his pockets, feeling for all the world like a little boy who had been caught with his hand in the cookie jar.

"Have you always been able to do this?"

"Yes."

"And why is it a secret? If you have this wonderful gift, you should be sharing it with everyone, like a doctor."

"I wish I could. Believe me, I help when I can, but society isn't really ready for people like me. I'd probably be locked up in some lab; poked and prodded and brought out to perform for special visitors. That's not how I want to spend my existence."

"I guess I can understand that, but how do you do it?"

He sighed, running his hands through his hair. "Steph, it's difficult to explain unless you know the whole story."

She folded her arms. "So tell me the whole story. I'm listening."

"I will, but you have to promise to keep an open mind and hear me out. Okay?"

"I promise. Cross my heart and hope to die."

"Don't say that. It's not funny!" He looked at her sharply, distressed at the very idea of her dying.

"Don't say what? Hope to die? It's just an expression." She gave him a look as if she doubted his sanity.

"Yes, but it strikes a bit too close to home for me. I've just found you. I can't lose you yet."

"You're not going to lose me, unless you can't explain this healing thing and why you have a file full of pictures of me."

He paced the room, running his hands through his hair, and then sat on the coffee table facing her. Taking her hands in his, he began. "You've heard stories of the ancient peoples and how they worshipped the gods? Beings that could do extraordinary things, who lived in the heavens and visited Earth?"

She nodded. "You mean like Greek mythology? Zeus and Hercules?"

"Something like that." He stared at their joined hands. "Well, what if I told you that those gods weren't just stories? That they did exist, but they weren't really gods, just a different race of beings. What if they were people who could travel the universe and that, after stumbling upon Earth, they decided to hang out here for a while?" He looked up, catching her eye. "Do you think that could have been possible?"

"Well... Maybe. I'm not totally into the idea of aliens or supernatural beings, but I try to keep an open mind." She nodded slowly.

"Okay. That's a start." He smiled, pleased she wasn't immediately discounting what he was saying. "Now consider the fact that some of these beings might have, er, interacted with the humans and had children who were half human but half 'god' as well. These hybrid offspring would have been special. Most would probably have been more like their human parent, but there would have been a few who took after the 'gods' in their abilities and life span." He paused and looked at her, gauging her reaction before continuing. "Stephanie, it's not just a story. It's true. It did happen, and I was one of the second group of children."

Stephanie burst out laughing and pulled her hands free of his. "What? Jake, I think you're a pretty great guy, but a 'god'? Quit joking around."

He shook his head. "Shh. You said you'd listen and I'm not joking. I, and others like me, grew up on Earth and became attached to the people and the way of life, while our parents eventually tired of humanity and moved on. Some of the children left as well, but not all. Some were incapable of changing into the form needed to leave, not having received the right genetic blend. Others, such as myself, could have left but chose not to. It wasn't a popular decision." He reached for her hand again but she pulled away, frowning. A heavy feeling settled in his stomach and he had to work to keep his voice steady. "The elders still keep trying to entice us away from here, but most of us have resisted. We've each found our own special 'incentive' that makes remaining more appealing and, as a result, have existed here for centuries, trying to blend in and live 'normal' lives."

She blinked, disbelief written all over her face. "So you're telling me that you're a gazillion years old?"

"Well, I'm not sure what a gazillion is, but by your standards yes, I'm old."

"You're pretty well preserved for an old guy." Sarcasm dripped from her voice.

He bit back a sigh. "Changing my appearance is just a quirky thing that I can do. It's sort of a survival skill, or a way to camouflage myself so I blend in with those around me. I can make myself look older or younger. I try to 'age' like those around me. Once I become 'old' I usually move before people become suspicious of my longevity." He shrugged. "Then I start over in a new location and make a new life for myself. I never go back to childhood since I'd have to find people to pose as parents. Twenty five is usually a good age to start a new life."

"Not that I believe any of this, but how old are you now, in this life?"

"My driver's licence says I'm thirty." He gave her a steady look, willing her to believe him.

Stephanie stood up and walked over to the balcony doors. She had her hands shoved into her back pockets. After a moment she turned, shaking her head in disbelief. "This is ridiculous. I can't believe I'm even asking you questions. The healer bit I can handle. Some people do have unusual abilities, but trying to believe that you're a 'god' who can live forever—"

"Not forever, Steph. I'm not immortal. One day my life force will run out and I'll die just like all living creatures do."

"I thought you'd died today..." Steph's voice trailed off as she relived the horror of the moment.

"By human standards I did, but I was just severely weakened. If it hadn't been for you, I might actually have just let myself drift away. The others—my family I guess you'd call them—wanted me to leave this life, but then I thought of you and I knew couldn't." He stood and faced her. "I managed to draw on some of the energy that forms the universe and pull myself back. It was difficult, but not impossible. My energy levels will need some time to stabilize which is why I was so upset when you left the van. If you'd been hurt, I probably wouldn't have been able to help you."

She rubbed her hands over her face and then looked at him. "Okay. I'm glad you're all right, really I am, and I don't claim to understand how you do it, but... All this other stuff? I don't know." She shook her head. "Why don't we just leave this hokey ancient god story behind for a bit and get down to why you have a thick file on me?"

"It's all intertwined. Come and sit down again. I'm trying to explain. It's just…complicated."

Stephanie gazed at him for a long moment, then sighed and came back to the sofa. "Okay. Lay it on me."

"Remember I said there were two groups of children. One group was more like the gods."

"And the others were more human. I remember."

He sat down beside her and was pleased when she didn't move away. "Well, the more human group did receive some of their parents' special qualities. They were usually more sensitive to the emotions and feelings of those around them, more intuitive; some might call it ESP or telepathy. Also, they don't just live and die, ceasing to exist on this plain as normal humans would do. Instead, their life force is attached to this solar system and even though they live and die, their spirit—for lack of a better word—remains and returns to this world." He took her hand and looked into her eyes. "Yours is one of those spirits, Steph. You've lived many lives. Of course you don't fully remember, but I do. Each time your spirit cycles back to life, I feel its return. We've been partners, soul mates, lovers—whatever you want to call it—for centuries."

Stephanie snorted. "Yeah, right.

"But why is that so hard to believe? Think about it. How many times have you had a déjà vu feeling? Thought you've seen or heard or done something before, even when you know you haven't—at least not in this life. Aren't you overly sensitive to the feelings or moods of those around you? Didn't you say you could 'feel' someone watching you?" He leaned forward, trying to put as much sincerity into his voice as possible, willing her to believe him. "And didn't you feel a connection to me when we met? Didn't you hear me talking to you while you were in the van? Haven't you wondered why, given your past experience, you so quickly came to trust me, to want to be with me? It's because our spirits know each other. They reach out to each other. Steph, we've known each other for thousands of years."

"Jake, I'm trying really hard to keep an open mind here, but this is pretty weird. I admit I did think I heard you—maybe even felt you—in the van, but that could have just been wishful thinking." She looked around the room as if hoping for inspiration on ways to challenge what he was telling her. "Okay, so explain to me, if you know my spirit has 'cycled back,' then, to coin a phrase, where have you been all my life?"

"Searching for you. I know you're back, but I never know where. I have to look for you, and as the world becomes more populated, it keeps getting harder."

"What? No crystal ball?" She arched a brow.

"Don't be sarcastic; I'm doing my best here." He felt his jaw tighten in frustration and willed himself to relax. This was difficult for her to take in—it challenged all she'd ever believed. Briefly, he longed for the days when the human mind was simpler and women more subservient. There'd been fewer difficult questions to answer back then. A mere century ago, Steph had meekly accepted whatever he told her. Oh, she'd fussed a bit—she'd always been spirited—but once he'd ended the conversation it had been over and done with. Being lord and master of the household had been so much easier than dealing with an independent, free-thinking woman but he'd adjust, just as he always did. It was important to keep up with the times. Sighing, he returned to answering her questions.

"No, I don't have those abilities since I'm only a hybrid. I just know you're here. It's a bit like that children's game where you get warmer or colder as you search for something. I sense when I'm closer to you or going farther away. Sometimes, in some of your lives, I've missed you completely. You've died young due to a plague or natural disaster, or there's been an accident or a war. If I'm with you, I can heal you, but if we're apart..." He shook his head sadly. "During the Second World War I missed you completely. It was so difficult to travel anywhere. I knew I was getting close. You were somewhere in Europe, but I didn't find you in time. One day you were there, and then suddenly I knew you were gone. Your village was probably bombed or, given how spirited you tend to be, you were working as a member of the Resistance. Either way, the result was the same. You'd been killed and I was alone again." He sighed heavily and looked away, remembering the pain and despair he'd experienced.

She reached out and touched his face. "That must have been very hard for you."

He turned and pressed a kiss to her palm. "Yeah, it was. That's why I was so excited to find you this time. We've been apart for over sixty years."

"Sixty? It seems like my 'spirit' is a little slow."

"I have no control over the forces that allow your spirit to come back. I just wait and live my life and hope. It's hard. Lonely. That's when I hear the voices in the night sky—my people calling to me, telling me to leave this planet and join them, but I know it would be an empty existence without you."

She cocked her head to the side. "Why don't you look for someone else, rather than waiting for me?"

"Because I only want you." He leaned forward and kissed her softly. She responded, but after a moment pulled away.

"So the pictures, the personal information you were gathering on me...?"

He shrugged. "Research. I've learned, over many lifetimes, that I can't just present myself to you and say 'here I am' or plug in our mental connection and start talking to you inside your head. I've made that mistake before, with disastrous results. I have to fit into your life, your culture. You have to get to know me, trust me, be willing to give yourself to me freely. Each time it's a new courtship."

Stephanie sat staring silently at their clasped hands. After a few minutes she looked up. "Jake, that's a pretty fantastic story, and I don't know how much of it I should believe or if you're just making up some fantasy world for reasons that I can't even begin to fathom. I need some time to think about this."

"About what I am or about us?"

"I'm not really sure. I guess both."

"All right. At least you're being honest. Would you like me to leave you alone for a while?"

"Well, it is your apartment but..." She nodded. He stood and looked down at her for a minute, then brushed his hand across her hair and left.

Chapter 23

Hearing the door close behind him, Stephanie flopped back on the sofa and contemplated the ceiling. This was insane. She'd just been held at gunpoint by a stalker, who was posing as her best friend's boyfriend, only to find out he was the same person who had attacked her nearly ten years ago. Then her own boyfriend appears to have supernatural healing powers, claims to be a half-breed alien and tells her that she is continually reincarnated so that they can always be together. And the really weird part? She'd sat there listening to him without calling the men in white suits to come and take him away. Was she going crazy or was it everyone around her?

A familiar weight landed on her stomach. Coco was walking up and down on top of her, kneading her paws to indicate that she needed attention and probably food. Coco had apparently finished sulking about being stuck in a carrier for half a day.

"Have you forgiven me for my vile treatment of you today?" The cat butted its head against her face, and Stephanie took that as a yes. She scooped the animal up and then got to her feet.

"You know, Coco, I think you're the only normal one around here. You're just you; a cat who got lucky and found a home. Now all you want out of life is three square meals a day, a clean litter box and the occasional scratch behind the ears. I wish my life was that simple."

She got out a can of cat food and put some in a dish, setting it on the floor for the impatient feline. Leaning back against the counter, she watched her pet eat and reflected how easily Coco had accepted Jake. She'd read somewhere that animals were good judges of character. Did that mean that Jake was trustworthy? She snorted derisively. Here she was considering the opinion of her cat. Maybe she was the one who was a bit loony tunes. She rubbed her forehead as thoughts and emotions swam around in her mind.

Maybe Jake was crazy and maybe she was too. Maybe the whole world was going off the deep end and did it even really matter? What it came down to was how she felt about Jake. Did his story change her feelings about him? She searched her heart and realized that he was still the same person she'd made love with last night. He was still kind and gentle, intelligent and funny, brave. So what if he had this one quirky idea? Was it so important that it negated everything else about him?

She felt a smile breaking out on her face as she realized the answer. Jake was Jake and she loved him for who he was right now, past lives or not.

And some of his story was true. The healing part she believed. After all, she'd seen the evidence with her own eyes when the knife wound had disappeared, but the rest, well, there was no way of proving or disproving it. All that existed was a file full of personal information about herself.

Pushing off from the counter, she headed to the bedroom to take another look at what he'd collected on her. The papers were still scattered all over the room, where she'd dropped them earlier. Bending down, she began to gather them together, skimming over some of the data as she went. It was quite comprehensive and accurate. Stacking it on the bed, she collected the pictures next, making a little moue over her appearance in some of them. She hated pictures of herself.

One was sticking out from under the edge of the bed and she tried to pick it up, but it seemed to be caught under something. On her hands and knees, she peered under the box spring to see what it was hooked on. Somehow it had snagged on the seam of a large metal box. She pulled the box out and worked the picture free, then started to push the box back only to pause when a single musical note came from inside. It sounded like a music box.

Intrigued, she pulled the metal container back out again. She loved music boxes and wondered what kind Jake might have. Lifting the latch, she paused, feeling a bit like Pandora, but then scoffed and peeked inside.

It appeared to be some kind of memory chest full of keepsakes and papers. A silver music box was sitting in the corner. She picked it up and admired the intricate carving then lifted the lid. A simple song started to play, the tune both familiar and haunting, though she couldn't put a name to it. She smiled as the delicate notes filled the room, then, when the song finished, she closed the lid and tipped it over to see if the song's name was on the bottom. There was no name but it was inscribed 'To Elizabeth, Love Thomas." She wondered who they might be. Possibly Jake's parents, if he did indeed have any.

Setting the music box down, she explored further. There was a gold plated hair brush, a string of pearls, a few letters, faded with age, in a language she couldn't read. Wrapped in tissue she found a framed portrait, the quality and the costumes of the occupants letting her know it was from the late 1800s. 'Natalia and Ivan – Moscow, 1883' was written on the back. A small painting of a woman was the next item she found. 'à Jean aime Maria - joyeux anniversaire, 30, mai 1815' was written on a small cardboard tag with hand-drawn flowers.

She studied the small portrait and noted the woman seemed vaguely familiar. There was something about her eyes, her smile... Carefully she picked up the photograph and studied it. It appeared to be the same woman, which was impossible given the dates. Possibly a grandmother? Peering at the photograph of the man, she realized that she was looking at a picture of Jake or at least his double. With her finger she traced the familiar jaw, nose and eyebrows. He was stern looking with longer hair as was the style for the time, but there was no mistaking that the man in the photo was Jake.

Could his story be true?

She took the picture into the bathroom and held the photo up so she could see it and herself at the same time. The hair was different, her lips were a bit fuller but the eyes, the cheek bones, the determined chin—they were all hers.

Carefully, she set the picture down and gripped the edge of the sink. Was Jake telling her the truth? Had she lived before or was it just some strange coincidence? It seemed incredible, but this appeared to be actual proof.

The sound of the apartment door had her rushing back to the bedroom, guiltily trying to restore the items to the metal chest before Jake discovered she'd been snooping. He called out her name and his footsteps came closer. She laid the photograph inside, put the music box back in, reached for the lid and started to flip it shut…

"Steph?" The bedroom door swung open and she turned to look just as the lid was coming down.

"Ow!" The metal top slammed on her hand. A thin line of blood appeared and she pulled her hand back wincing as the nerve endings throbbed. She squeezed her eyes tightly shut, rocking back and forth as the waves of pain shot up her arm, making her feel slightly faint and queasy.

"Steph! What happened? Where are you hurt?"

"My hand! The lid fell on it. I think I broke a finger or something.

"Let me see." He took her hand and gently cradled it in his own. Almost immediately, the pain subsided. She opened her eyes and stared in wonder as the cut faded away as well, right before her eyes. Experimentally, she wiggled her fingers in his hand. There was no pain, no discomfort. It was as if the lid had never fallen on it at all.

"Jake, that really is amazing. If I hadn't experienced it, I wouldn't have believed it. I mean I did believe you because of what happened at Ella's but... Wow! To just watch it happen." She gazed up at him in wonder and then surprise as her brain finally began to connect events together. "Hey! That's what happened to my paper cut, and the allergies and the sunburn."

He nodded and then his gaze drifted to the metal box. She felt herself flush, embarrassed at having been caught prying into his personal things.

"I discovered this under the bed and umm, I was sort of looking inside."

Jake lifted the lid and checked the contents, reverently touching and rearranging them to his satisfaction.

"I'm sorry. I shouldn't have been snooping. I was picking up the pictures I dropped earlier and one had slipped under the bed. It was stuck under the edge of this box. When I moved it, I heard the music box chime a note and I was just going to take a little peek."

Jake picked up the music box, carefully wound it before opening the lid. The simple notes drifted between them. "You always loved this." He held it out to her. "Here, it's yours."

Surprised, she stared at it, keeping her hands in her lap. "Mine? You can't give this to me. It's a keepsake and probably worth a fortune from the looks of it."

He shrugged. "I gave it to you once before, for our tenth anniversary. You always said it was your favourite out of all the things I'd ever given you."

"Our tenth anniversary?" She frowned. "Oh. You mean in one of those other lives you were talking about." She shifted uncomfortably, still not sure what to think.

"It's all right, Steph. You don't have to believe me." He looked a little sad and carefully closed the lid. The music stopped and he placed it back in the metal box.

She felt guilty for hurting him, confused, unsure. Licking her lips, she quietly asked, "Jake, are all of these things keepsakes of our lives together?"

"Yes. Each time you've...died, I've kept one or two trinkets to remind me of you. They comfort me while you're gone."

"Some of these things look really old and expensive."

"Some of them are. Others are only significant to me. Someday, I'll tell you about each of them, if you want." He looked at her questioningly, a faint flicker of hope evident in his eyes.

"That would be nice."

He smiled at her and carefully closed the box then slid it back under the bed. They both stood and stared at each other awkwardly, neither seeming to know what to say.

Finally Stephanie spoke. "Jake, about what you told me earlier—the healing and the multiple lives and stuff—I've been thinking and..." She shrugged. "I guess it doesn't really matter to me if you believe that or not."

"So, in other words, you don't believe me."

"I didn't say that. What I meant was that I was thinking, and I've come to realize that you're still the same person you were when I met you, and whether any of this is true or not, I... I still love you." She stretched out her hand and placed it over his heart.

"You do? You love me?" She nodded and was immediately swept up in his arms. "Oh Steph, that's what I've been waiting decades to hear again. You don't know how happy you've just made me."

"I think I might have a slight idea if the strength of your grip is any indication."

"Oops, sorry!" He set her down, but kept his arms wrapped around her waist. "I was worried that you'd think I was crazy and refuse to see me again."

She gave him a quizzical look. "Could that happen, if we're destined to always be together?"

He nodded. "Once, in the Dark Ages, you thought I was an evil sorcerer. You were using garlic and hexes to keep me away." He chuckled. "The human factor can throw a monkey wrench into even the best laid plans. That's one of the things that frustrated my people the most and finally convinced them to leave. Humans were too independent and unpredictable."

"But you stuck it out?"

"Only because of you." He brushed his lips over her forehead, her eyes and along the curve of her cheek before finally reaching her mouth. Gently, almost reverently, he kissed her. "I love you, Stephanie."

"I know." She ran her hands over his shoulders. "I'm still a bit unsure about this whole multiple lives thing, but some of the stuff in that box is starting to convince me. Regardless, I do love you and I'll continue loving you for the rest of my life, whether it's just this one or, well... You know what I mean."

He nodded in understanding. Reaching up, she slowly traced his features as if rediscovering something once known but long forgotten. Tentatively, she outlined his eyebrows, cheeks and jaw. His eyes closed and he trembled faintly under her delicate touch. Her hands moved down to his shoulders and chest, her touch becoming surer, bolder. Something niggled in the back of her mind, a memory, a sense of having done this before."

She unbuttoned his shirt, and then smoothed it from his shoulders. Her eyes gazed upon the muscular plane of his chest, and her hands ran over it, exploring, teasing…

Replacing her hands with her mouth, she tasted the slight saltiness of his skin and inhaled the scent that was uniquely him. He drew in a ragged breath and she could hear the sound rumbling in his throat. It was all so familiar, her senses *knew* him. As she nipped lightly at his collarbone, his control broke and she was swept up in his arms.

They tumbled onto the bed and became lost in each other. Clothing was quickly shed as hands explored soft supple flesh, sliding down and then up over hills and valleys. Kisses, butterfly soft, feathered over her neck, her jaw, her cheeks. Warm breath teased her ear as words of love and desire spilled from his lips before his mouth captured hers, hot and urgent. Passion intensified and an all-consuming hunger grew within her, as if something inside her was finally being set free. This was Jake, her lover, her destiny. Need began to build inside her. Suddenly she couldn't get enough of him. The scent of him, the taste of him, the feel of him... She wanted to consume him, to be consumed *by* him.

And then, in that one moment, a light seemed to go on inside her mind and she caught his head with her hands, her gaze catching his. "Jake—I know! Somehow, something inside me knows. Everything you said, it's all true! I feel like a part of me was missing, sleeping, and now you've brought it to life."

"Oh God, Stephanie, I've missed you." His mouth crushed hers and a strange disembodiment began to take over. She was no longer just Stephanie Fields. Maria, Natalia, Elizabeth—everyone she had ever been seemed to be merging into one as she and Jake became lost in their love…

In the aftermath, they lay in each other's arms, idly caressing, sharing soft kisses. "Jake?"

"Hmm?"

"Does it always happen like this?"

"Yeah. It's always good between us." He hugged her closer.

"No—I meant that suddenly I seemed to know everything that had ever happened in the past. I wasn't just me, Stephanie, anymore. It didn't last though. Already it's kind of hazy, almost like a dream that fades away even as you try to recall it."

"Sometimes memories live on in the subconscious and, under the right circumstances, they resurface for a while."

"I like these circumstances."

"Mmm... Me, too."

She was quiet for a while, contemplating, and then spoke softly. "So, if memories live on in our subconscious, Stephanie Fields will never really be gone. I'll exist in the memory of some future me."

"And in my memory as well. You'll be a part of me forever."

"Forever?"

"Yes. Forever in time.

"I like that idea." She pressed a kiss to his lips. "I love you Jake."

"I love you too, Steph."

And as they drifted off to sleep in each other's arms, both knew their love was indeed going to last forever in time.

Epilogue

Jake lay in bed, with Stephanie cradled in his arms. Her warm breath fanned across his chest, her legs intertwined with his. It felt so good to be together again, to feel whole again. It had been an eventful day—too eventful for his liking. For a few moments, he'd actually wondered if they would even have their future together, but thankfully everything had worked out and all the ends were nicely tied up, except…

A faint frown marred his brow as he thought back to one particular instant. The police had just taken Jarrod and Murray away. Steph and Ella had been chatting and he'd been half listening, when suddenly he'd become aware of another mind touching his. It had just skimmed over, not really delving for information, almost as if the person controlling it wasn't totally versed in telepathic principles.

He knew there were more of his kind roaming the Earth. On rare occasions they would encounter each other, but for the most part there was no connection between them. They did not seek each other out unless dire circumstances required it. Was this presence one of his kind, a purebred or even a hybrid such as himself? It was unique, yet familiar.

Looking around, he'd probed those near him. It wasn't something he often did. Examining another's thoughts was both an invasion of privacy and disturbing. Being privy to someone's darkest thoughts or deepest secrets was not an easy thing to deal with. True, his mind connected with Stephanie's, but they were bonded and for them it was an act of intimacy.

Finally, he'd settled on a young police officer who had been crossing the lawn, heading towards Paula. There had been something about him, but then, just as he'd started to focus in on the man, Ella had spoken and the opportunity was lost.

Shifting slightly, he hugged Stephanie closer and rested his chin on her head. Possibly, he'd imagined the brief telepathic connection. It could have just been the aftermath of his close call that afternoon. After all, he'd never come that close to 'dying' before. Who knew what effects it might have had on him?

He considered the situation again and then dismissed it from his mind. What were the chances of encountering someone like himself? It must have been his mind playing tricks on him. Closing his eyes, he sighed happily and drifted off to sleep.

~FIN~

A Message from Nicky

Hi!

Thank you for reading my book. If you enjoyed it, please leave a review at your favourite retailer.

Forever In Time was the first original story I'd ever written. This is the re-edited and revised version. I tried to stay true to the original tale, though I did find that my writing style has evolved considerably since those early days! I've left this story open for a possible next book; I just need to find the time to sit down and write it!

~ Nicky

Connect with Me:

Email: nicky@nickycharles.com
Or nicky.charles@live.ca

At my website:
http://www.nickycharles.com

Follow me on Facebook:
https://www.facebook.com/NickyCharles

Books by Nicky Charles

Forever In Time

The Law of the Lycans series by Nicky Charles

The Mating

The Keeping

The Finding

Bonded

Betrayed: Days of the Rogue

Betrayed: Book 2 – The Road to Redemption

For the Good of All

Deceit can be Deadly

Kane: I am Alpha

Veil of Lies

Hearts & Halos

(Written with Jan Gordon)

In The Cards

Untried Heart

Lightning Source UK Ltd.
Milton Keynes UK
UKHW020013170123
415453UK00003B/38/J